FISTS

PIETRO GROSSI

FISTS

Translated from the Italian
by Howard Curtis

PUSHKIN PRESS
LONDON

www.pushkinpress.com

English translation © Howard Curtis 2009

First published in Italian as
Pugni © Sellerio editore 2006

This edition first published in 2009 by
Pushkin Press
12 Chester Terrace
London NW1 4ND

Reprinted 2010 (twice)

Supported by the National Lottery through
Arts Council England

This book is published with the support of the
Italian Ministry of Foreign Affairs.

British Library Cataloguing in Publication Data:
A catalogue record for this book is available
from the British Library

ISBN 978 1 906548 38 4

Cover: *Quatre Temps* 2004
© Alfons Alt

Frontispiece: Pietro Grossi

Set in 11 on 13.5 Monotype Baskerville
and printed in Great Britain on Munken Print 80 gsm
by MPG Books Ltd

LOTTERY FUNDED

Contents

To those who were there,
and still are

BOXING

L ET'S GET THIS STRAIGHT: I really liked the whole boxing thing.

I don't know what it was, whether it was the sense of security or the awareness that I was doing something the way it should be done. Maybe both, maybe also the terrific feeling that there was a place where I had what it takes, where I could fight on equal terms.

There was a logic about it. You couldn't escape it, neither you nor anyone else; you knew who you were fighting, it was always a single person, he weighed as much as you did, and if he beat you that meant he was either better than you or more experienced, and in both cases all you could do was learn from your defeat. I know it seems absurd, but the fact is, you end up going to a place where everyone fights because you feel more secure there.

There was also the fact that I was good at it. It must have been all those videos of Muhammad Ali and Sugar Ray Robinson my dad used to watch when I was little, but when I walked into that hangar-like building for the first time and saw that patched-together ring, which was only standing by a miracle, I imagined myself up there skipping about like Ali and firing off jabs like arrows.

I don't know, maybe if you convince yourself of something, in the end you get it. The fact is, that's how I learnt to fight: I would skip around my opponent and torment him like a mosquito with those straight punches as precise and quick and sharp as strokes of a lash. Let's be honest: I didn't have a boxer's body, I didn't look very promising. I was skinny, with a long, straight neck, slender wrists, thin legs and bony knees. I looked like a branch

13

hurriedly stripped of its twigs. But I got up there, hunched my shoulders, raised my guard, started hopping backwards and forwards, and it was as if I was getting ready to fly. Sometimes I thought I heard Beethoven, a piano sonata maybe, and I had the feeling I was inside that deaf bastard's notes, landing straight punches to the rhythm of the music.

It was my mother who had forced me to learn the piano. She made me take lessons from a filthy old woman whose breath stank and who scattered dandruff like confetti.

That was how I started boxing. I was the perfect son— studious, nerdy, conventional, obedient, who went to bed early and who, if you asked him, even said his prayers before going to sleep. But he didn't want to play the piano. I hated the piano. I hated Mozart and Bach and that deaf freak Beethoven and that stinky old woman, Signora Poli. The only one I could swallow a bit was Rachmaninov, because the music always sounded angry and because it was so hard to play.

One day, I told my mother I hated the piano. Music was fundamental, she said, it gave you discipline. Discipline. Why discipline? I was the most disciplined child in the world. I was so disciplined, I'd almost vanished from the face of the earth.

My mother looked at me and told me not to talk nonsense, music was important. It was a tricky situation.

"Then I also want to learn to box."

"What?"

"If I play the piano I also want to learn to box."

"To box?"

"That's right, to box."

"Don't talk nonsense," my mother said, trying to cut the conversation short.

"I want to learn to box."

"The word *want* doesn't cut any ice with me."

It was the first time I had dug my heels in with my mother, and half-of-me felt strangely excited, as if I had suddenly woken up and landed a left-right in the sixth round of a tough fight. The other half-of-me wanted to cry.

"I want to learn to box." Right hook to the face.

"Let's not even talk about it. Discussion closed."

End of round. Saved by the bell.

But I'd woken up, I'd raised my head high. For once, the nice, disciplined little boy was fighting for something. It was a difficult fight; one of those exhausting fifteen-round matches. I stopped studying, kept my mouth shut for two oral tests in a row, stopped speaking and playing the piano. Three times Signora Poli had to give up after trying for ten minutes to make me play or speak. She had even convinced herself to feel sorry for me. I went a whole week without speaking. No one knew what to do; they were ready to send me to a shrink, when one evening my mother suddenly came into my bedroom and told me she'd talked to my father, and that if I wanted I could try boxing.

"Good," I said. "I'll enrol at the gym tomorrow."

It was my first victory: a technical knockout in the fourteenth round, prepared with skill and patience. Maybe I would have won on points anyway. I don't know, my mother has always been a bit of a pain.

When I enrolled, a couple of boys started laughing, and Gustavo, a thin old guy with a voice like a black jazzman, asked me to bring certificates and authorisation from my parents, statements absolving the gym of responsibility and five thousand lire for the registration fee.

Six months later, I was dancing in that ring like a ballerina and scattering straight lefts like summer hailstones. It was undeniable: even though no one had ever seen a boxer with a more unsuitable body, it was if I was born to be up there. And since I'd started training, my piano playing had improved, too, and I was even starting to like that bastard Beethoven. I don't know what happened to me up there, but suddenly the noises, the shouts and the smells would disappear, the world around me would disappear and all I saw was my opponent, who suddenly seemed almost to be moving in slow motion, all I heard was my own heartbeat, as clear and regular as a steam train. Only my heartbeat and the tired eyes of the poor guy in front of me.

Left. Left. Turn, skip. Left. Left. Left right left. Turn. Parry. Parry. Left. Parry. Left right left. Left. Turn. Turn. Skip. Sharp right and left hook. Bell.

I was a pleasure to watch. Gustavo showed me off to everyone as if I was a new car.

"Try to guess how much he weighs," he would ask people who didn't know me, his eyes all lit up like a boy's, as if he was asking them about his car. "Try to guess how many kilometres to the litre."

"I don't know, sixty-six kilos, maybe sixty-seven?" they would usually say.

Gustavo would give one of his black jazzman's half-laughs. "Sixty-three and a half," he would say. "A junior welterweight."

Then he would send me into the ring and tell me to go one round. While I was up there, dancing, he would nudge that friend of his who had never seen me and smile.

"My dear Giorgi," I heard him say once to a guy in a long wet raincoat, "we're going to get this one to the Olympics."

"Why not let him turn pro?" the other man asked.

"That nose doesn't deserve it," Gustavo replied.

I do in fact have quite a nice nose. It stands out like a smooth, well-drawn little mountain on that hollow, lop-sided face of mine, looking as if it's been removed from someone else's face and stuck there—but, although it doesn't really fit, it seems to give some kind of order to the rest.

I don't know why Gustavo had convinced himself that if I stayed an amateur my nose would be saved, as if amateurs threw fewer punches. The fact is that, when he told that guy Giorgi that he would take me to the Olympics, I hadn't had a single fight.

I was a kind of legend. They talked about me in all the gyms. They called me the Dancer. Quite often, some boxer shooting his mouth off, who might not even have seen me, would actually call me the Ballerina. It was said I was the best, the strongest, and that I didn't fight because I knew I'd already won. They said a whole lot of things, and people went crazy talking about me. The trainers cursed because I could have taken gold for Italy at the Olympics but wasn't interested; the local toughs talked about me on the streets without even having seen me, and the boxers, when they weren't shooting their mouths off, were grateful that I didn't fight and hoped I would carry on like that.

It was a nice feeling: sometimes some man or boy would visit the gym and after a while I would see Gigi, the other trainer, point at me. They would take a few steps and stand there looking self-conscious like someone coming in to see a head of state, and they always stopped for a few minutes and watched me train. God knows what they later told other people. Apparently one day a schoolmate told his friends that I was the Dancer, that he had seen me in the gym.

"Who?"

"That guy who always dresses like a nerd and carries a leather satchel."

"The one wandering off alone over there?"

"Yes."

17

"Fuck off."

"I swear!"

"Get away!"

"I know it for certain, I saw him yesterday in the gym, you should have seen how fast he was."

"I wouldn't believe it even if I saw him."

No one doubted that I would win against any of the guys around me, not even me. It didn't take much to realise that that clumsy, clodhopping bunch who wasted most of their punches were powerless against a lean, winged animal that danced in the ring like a butterfly.

God knows what they would have thought if they had known that I didn't fight because my mother didn't want me to, what they would have said if they had known that behind my mysterious, fascinating reluctance stood the slender figure of my mother, that apparently inoffensive lady whose hair was already starting to turn white. They wouldn't have believed it. Or else they would have split their sides laughing and I would always have remained 'the Ballerina', however many punches I landed, however many titles I won, however many Olympics I competed in.

Every now and again, though, things happen to you that change your life. And then you want to turn back the clock and say no, I liked it better the way it was before. But the vase is broken and whatever was inside is now on the table, gradually drying, and showing the world as it really is, with a bit of colour, maybe, but the way it is. One day, you see the anger and discover what sweat is.

I only fought once in my life. I mean seriously. Referee, corner, audience, bets and all the rest of it. People still remember it. There are still some who say it was the best fight they ever saw.

I HAD ONLY SEEN HIM FIGHT ONCE. There was a big fight meeting at the Teatro Tenda, and I went with Beppe. I told mother the school was taking us to see a play by Pirandello. She swallowed it, so I got my friend Beppe to pick me up outside my house and give me a lift on his old three-colour Ciao moped which was always so difficult to start. He was one of the few people at school who knew about this boxing business, but somehow he didn't want to believe that I was really good. I think he thought I'd made it all up, that I didn't even go to the gym, that it was all a fantasy in order to make me seem less of a nerd than I was. The first time he started to suspect it might be true was when he came over to my place one afternoon to study and on the way we got caught in a downpour and ended up as soaked as dishcloths. We undressed in my room, which wasn't something that happened often, because I didn't have many friends. Anyway, Beppe and I were in the bedroom when I heard him cry out, "Bloody hell!"

I looked up and saw that he was looking at me with a stupid half-smile on his face.

"What is it?" I said.

"Fuck," he said. "What a body."

I looked down at those prominent pectorals, those chequered stomach muscles and those sinewy arms. When I was dressed, you'd never have guessed that beneath those trousers and those over-large nerdy shirts there was that knot of muscles, small but nice and taut.

"Thanks," I said.

"But how do you do it?"

"I told you, I box."

19

"Yeah, right."

I didn't care if he didn't believe it. Outside the gym, I usually didn't believe it myself. Outside the gym, everyone made fun of me, I never had a girlfriend, always said the wrong thing, got good marks, played the piano and didn't have a moped, and so even I ended up forgetting that there was a damp, stinking place where I was a sensation.

After the night of the fight meeting, though, all Beppe's doubts vanished. It was as if I was back in my world, even though it was outside the gym. There was the Finger tearing tickets at the entrance—the same Finger who'd got out of prison six months earlier, the same Finger I'd been telling how to deliver decent hooks a couple of weeks before.

He saw me from a distance at the back of the queue and started waving his arms.

"Hey, skinny! What are you doing back there? Come here, I'll let you through!"

We squeezed through the other people and when we got to the front the Finger smiled and shook my hand and slapped me on the back a couple of times and told me how pleased he was that I had come.

"This is Beppe, a friend of mine," I said, and the Finger shook his hand, too. Still smiling, he told us to go through.

Inside, there were lots of people going back and forth under the neon lights, between the bar and the red curtains which led to the stalls.

Beppe and I had two cokes at the bar as if they were bourbon on the rocks and went into the stalls. The symmetrical fortress of the ring rose like a wedding cake under the spotlights.

One by one, the guys from the gym came up to me and greeted me. They hugged me, slapped me on the back and greeted Beppe as if he were one of the gang. And during the fights they nudged me with their elbows every now and again and said, "You should be up there." Which wasn't, in fact, a bad idea: I could easily see myself up there under those spotlights, dancing around an opponent, covering him with straight punches like mosquito bites, and then in the end having my hand lifted by the referee to thunderous applause, or looking down at the other man lying on the ground after a good straight right to the chin.

But my mother didn't want that, damn her, so there I sat, watching the fights, content with the certainty that I would have won and the slaps on the back from my pals and the glances from Beppe, who was starting to look on me as a bit of a legend.

Whether they won or lost, the kids up there in the ring were all small-timers. All awkward, lumbering guys completely lacking in class. With one exception: the Goat.

He got up in the ring with those eyebrows of his hanging over his eyes like kitbags. As he sat there in the corner, with a towel round his shoulders, he held his dark-red gloves close to his chin, moved his head from side to side and hit himself on the jaw as if to remind himself that he'd soon be taking punches. I sensed immediately that he was good, that he was in a different class.

I leant over to Giano, a tall, well-built young guy with the body of a swimmer who was pretty scary in the ring but was too crazy to fight.

"Who's that?" I asked.

Giano turned and looked at me in surprise. "That's Mugnaini, the Goat."

"That's the Goat?"

"Yes, that's him."

"I didn't know he was fighting tonight."

"Neither did I."

I sat back again in my seat and watched him skipping in the corner, while his second massaged his shoulders.

"Who's the Goat?" Beppe asked.

I couldn't take my eyes off him. "Someone who's never lost a fight," I said, lost in thought.

Beppe looked at him for a few seconds then turned to me again. "And why's he called the Goat?"

I leant forwards and placed my elbows on my knees. "Because he always keeps moving forwards with his head down," I said.

Beppe nodded again. I couldn't stop staring at him. It was as if his skipping and the streak of shadow under his eyebrows had hypnotised me and dragged me up there into the ring to get a closer look at him, to see if I could find out whether, in that darkness beneath his forehead, somewhere behind those eyes, there was someone who could beat me.

"He's a deaf mute," I said.

Apparently, no one had noticed at first. He was only a strange, rather silent, solitary boy who didn't take up much space in the gym. He always arrived on time for his training, changed without looking at anyone, was always last in the queue for warming up, and whenever Buio, the trainer, explained a technique, he would always stand a little back from the others, his eyes as sombre and dark as TV cameras—but he'd record everything and then get down to it until he'd grasped it, practising again and again, probably practising at home by himself, too. Right after right, left after left, hook after hook, like a machine.

It was Masi who discovered he was a deaf mute. Masi was a tall, slim guy, the son of a gravedigger, a typical street kid, a bit of a hooligan, who liked beating up smaller kids as they came out of the football stadium. He was a decent middleweight, agile and confident, maybe the great white hope of the gym at the time. Just then, he was in training for the Italian championships, which he would lose in the semi-finals to a young guy from Bergamo who was as hard as a mule.

The Goat was working out at the punchbag, and Masi couldn't find another one free. It wasn't right that the aspiring Italian champion, beginners' class, should have to cool his heels waiting to go a couple of rounds at the punchbag. He stood behind him and waited for the Goat to finish his round. When the bell on the big grey clock which hung on the dirty wall at the back of the room rang at the end of the four minutes, Masi said he needed the punchbag. He was on his feet, loosening up his neck and punching the air lightly to relax his arms. The Goat did not reply.

"Hey," Masi said, raising his voice. "I need the bag."

But the Goat still didn't respond. He stood there in front of the punchbag, like a brawny little Roman in front of a column.

"HEY," Masi cried, raising his voice even more. "I NEED THE BAG."

Everyone stopped, and those who saw the Goat from the front realised that he had his eyes closed. Masi looked at his pals, shrugged his shoulders and smiled, as if to say, "What is this guy, an idiot?" Then he made his mistake, he did something that anyone who'd been around the block a bit would advise you not to do in a boxing gym: he picked a quarrel. He brought both his gloves down on the Goat's shoulders, sending him thudding into the punchbag like a skier into a tree. Masi barely had time to see him turn before the short, squat, fair-haired boy was under him. Two feints, then a left, a right and a left, and Masi was on the ground, stunned, and that squat, fair-haired boy was standing over him whinnying like a horse and looking as if he was spitting fire from his nostrils. Masi got back on his feet, smiling.

"So you want to do this the hard way," Masi said. He took off his stinking punchbag gloves, leaving only the bandages on. "Come on," he said. He fired off two lefts at the Goat's head, but the Goat parried and turned with his fists up and his head down. There was Masi, tall and slim, his arms and shoulders going up and down like in a documentary on boxing, and there was the other guy in front of him, all hunched and as closed up as a ball of granite. A left and a right from Masi. The Goat saw that long, sharp right before it had even started on its journey. He bent his knees, parried to the left, moved forwards and, pressing down with the full weight of his body, fired off one more of those millions of uppercuts to the liver that he'd been practising in the last few weeks. He saw, as if it was lit up, that uncovered area of the body where Buio had said the liver was and which brings everyone down. And, as if it was all one move, the Goat followed it with a short right to the chin and a left hook to the temple. There are those who are ready to swear they saw Masi leave the ground before he went flying into the punchbag, and then he was down, flat on the ground, and unconscious for five minutes. Masi weighed twelve kilos more than the Goat, and was almost twenty-five centimetres taller. Buio came running and pushed the Goat away, insulting him as he did so. Everyone crowded around Masi, ignoring the young sensation, not even hearing the weak "I'm sorry" muttered by someone who had obviously never learnt to speak.

A couple of days later, a short, plump woman wearing a man's hat came to the gym and asked for the owner. Someone went to fetch Buio.

"Hello, I'm Sonia Mugnaini."

"Hello, I'm Buio."

"Good evening, Signor Buio. I've come to ask you to take my son back for training. The thing is, this is the first time I've seen him really interested in something. Everyone always makes fun of him and I know he's not particularly bright, but deep down he's a lovely boy. He's had a hard life and he's always alone and—"

"One moment, signora. I don't know what you're talking about."

"Oh." Signora Mugnaini was puzzled. "He told me he can't come back because he hit someone. You have to forgive him, it won't happen again. It's just that, you know, he gets these attacks, but maybe you could try to understand, maybe—"

"Signora, just stop there. Are you the mother of that fair-haired boy?"

"Yes, of course, who did you think I was talking about?"

"You know, signora, a lot of boys come here, and they're always hitting each other, one way or another."

The man had a point, Signora Mugnaini thought.

"Anyway, signora, your son can come back whenever he likes. Your son is very talented."

"Didn't you throw him out?"

"No. Of course, I don't want him beating up all my boys."

Signora Mugnaini let out a laugh. "Yes, you're right," she said. "It's just that he didn't hear, you know how it is—"

"He didn't hear?"

"Well, I should have thought that was obvious."

"Not really. I heard, and I was in my office."

Signora Mugnaini again gave Buio a puzzled look. "I'm sorry, Signor Buio, but in six months haven't you noticed that my son is a deaf mute?"

25

One evening a few months earlier, while watching an old Dean Martin film, it had occurred to Buio that it had been a long time since he had last felt embarrassed. And he had come to the conclusion that maybe that's one of the things you acquire as you get older: you have your work, you're well respected, you have a bit of a paunch but two big arms and a mean look, and the bad old days when life wrong-footed you and landed you in embarrassing situations have long gone. You get backache sometimes, you need to have your prostate checked, the other day one of your knees turned to jelly, but you don't have to worry any more about being embarrassed. And then life comes along, in the form of a cylinder-shaped lady in a man's hat, and slaps you in the face, right there, right where you're at home, where you're the boss, everyone looks on you as a master, everyone respects you when you shout at them in your loud voice and everyone likes it when you pat them on the back. Life takes the form of a mother and leaves you stunned. And makes you turn red like a little boy.

"A deaf mute?"

"I'm sorry again, Signor Buio." Signora Mugnaini's voice had assumed a very slightly ironic tone. "My son has been coming here for six months, three times a week, four if he has time. I even bought him a punchbag for his room. And you never noticed he's a deaf mute?"

Buio looked at the lady, his back stooped. The skin of his face suddenly dropped, as if someone had attached dozens of weights to it.

"Well, no," he said. "I'm sorry, I didn't notice, no one noticed. You know how it is."

"No, I don't know how it is." Signora Mugnaini's tone was decidedly sarcastic now.

"It's just that he's always by himself, away from the others, always quiet … "

"That's because he can't speak."

Buio thought it best not to say anything else, not to clutch at straws, because he was already embarrassed enough to feel as if he'd been taken forty years back in time. His back was even more stooped, as if the caretaker, without being seen, had put two ten-kilo sacks in his hands.

"I'm sorry," Buio said in a thin voice, with his head bowed.

"That's all right, Signor Buio. I know my son is a very reserved boy, and that can fool people. I understand how difficult that can be. But maybe you should pay more attention to your boys."

Buio nodded with his head bowed, and for a moment met Signora Mugnaini's stern, determined eyes.

"Goodbye, Signor Buio."

"Goodbye, signora."

I don't know if it was as a reaction to that embarrassment, or out of compassion or admiration, or because of the Goat's sheer, obvious talent, but from that day on Buio's attitude changed to that squat, fair-haired boy with the forehead like a wall and the shadow over his eyes that looked like a mask. He took him under his wing and turned him into a great boxer. The boy's talent was second only to his dedication, and perhaps to Buio's enthusiasm, as he watched him grow from day to day in his hands.

As the weeks passed, he saw everything take shape: those shoulders along with that perfect left hook, that sculpted back along with that granite guard, the line of those pectorals along with that perfect legwork. The Goat was a sponge, a machine for learning, and within barely a year he was ready for his first fight. He won the regional championships, beginners' class, then the national championships, in the finals of which, in a mere forty-eight seconds, he saw off a bull-headed Milanese who everyone considered a great white hope.

By the time I saw him fighting that night at the Teatro Tenda he had cleaned up in the first heats of the national championships for two years running, and was preparing for the European championship. His opponent was a slim boy with catlike eyes who came from a village near Rome. He was a decent boxer, quick on his feet, and defended himself well. Sooner or later, he intended to strip the Goat of his growing legend. He knew it wouldn't be that night, there was no point in even trying. The Goat had agreed to the fight because it was good practice, and the Roman boy because he wanted to see him at work, at close quarters, without much risk to himself. One of these days, he'd fight him properly and beat him. But that night he didn't manage to land a single punch. The Goat would wait for Buio to hit him on the leg to let him know that the bell had gone, then, like a machine, he would raise his guard, put his head inside his gloves, hunch his shoulders and skip to the centre of the ring, just like a goat. The Roman boy did what he could: he kept firing off lefts and rights, one after the other, trying to keep that squat little animal with the shadow over his eyes at a distance. But he didn't even hit him once. It was like a game: making little movements with his body and bending his knees, the Goat managed to parry all those straight punches, one after the other, as if he knew when and how they were coming. And those he didn't parry he let run on, brushing them away with his glove as if they were mosquitoes. That was all he did for two rounds. Two frustrating rounds during which I saw the tension rising on his opponent's face, punch after punch; two frustrating rounds during which the Roman boy's punches, sharp and clean at first, turned loose and messy. It had become a matter of honour to him to hit the Goat at least once, but the Goat just watched as he became ever more flustered. By the end of the second round, the boy was tired, worn down by his own powerlessness, and his once accurate punches simply piled up on top of each other, obsessively, leaving him as wide open as a valley.

In the third round, the Goat made a beeline for that valley like a ploughman who'd rested well and had a good lunch. Fresh as a rose, he would wait for one of his opponent's messy punches and would get in there with a lightning-fast one-two-three combination. Parry, parry, parry, bend to the left, uppercut, straight punch, hook, swivel and step back. Pause, then parry, parry to the right, hook, uppercut, hook, swivel and step back. He was a pleasure to watch.

After the fifth combination, the Roman boy staggered back onto the ropes and stayed there, and the referee started counting. His trainer went to him, examined him, and stopped the fight.

For the first time I had seen a boxer who could beat me. It was a hard blow. On the way home that night, I couldn't say a word. When we got to my front door I almost forgot to say goodnight to Beppe.

"Hey," he said as I unlocked the door.

I turned, lost in thought. "Hey," I replied.

"Goodnight, then."

"Goodnight."

"What's the matter?"

"Nothing. I'm tired."

I was just about to go inside.

"He was good, wasn't he?" Beppe said, already with his feet on the pedals, ready to start his moped. I thought about it for a moment. I wished I could play it down and say "Not bad".

"Yes, he's good," I replied.

T HE WORLD CHANGED. Suddenly there was someone out there capable of beating me, or at least of having a good shot at it.

Up until then, I'd been such a nerd, the only thing I didn't do was collect stamps. But that was fine, there was even something quite appealing about the fact that there was that one place which was like a distorting mirror. From that point of view, my life was actually rather amazing: I felt like an undercover CIA agent, a character from a film with a double life I had to keep secret. I looked at all the boys who considered me a nerd and thought, *you don't know.* I almost felt like a superhero, Spiderman or something. I was Peter Parker and Clark Kent.

But now, suddenly, I had realised that it was all in my imagination, that I wasn't the best or the strongest, that the world was a big place and there were probably loads of people better than me. In other words, the chances that I was a superhero had suddenly become very slim.

That was why, when I found out that Buio had gone to see Gustavo and asked him to let me fight, I jumped for joy.

Apparently, one afternoon, the Goat had gone to Buio and tossed a piece of paper on his desk. Buio had looked up, puzzled, and had picked up the paper. On it, the words '*I want to fight the Dancer*' were written.

Buio dropped the paper on the desk and the first thing that came into his mind was "Why?" But he knew why, and perhaps he didn't want to hear the answer repeated. Buio knew these things, and he didn't like them. He knew what it meant not to be sure whether you were the strongest or not. And he knew how, in the ring, that uncertainty could become an obsession.

The second thing that came into Buio's mind was "How does he know about the Dancer?"

The first time the Goat had seen that name was on the lips of Mirco, a mediocre heavyweight who had somehow managed to win a regional championship, beginners' class, before becoming a plumber and ending up in prison for robbery. He saw that sequence of syllables *dan-cer, dan-cer* appear, almost in slow motion, on Mirco's coarse lips, and immediately they rang in his head like a bell. The Goat couldn't follow the conversation very well, because Mirco and the other two guys, who were drying themselves after the showers, kept moving and turning away, but he had the impression they were talking about a fight: the heavyweight's lopsided eyes excitedly echoed the avalanche of words which seemed to gush from his mouth like a fountain, and from time to time he raised his guard, fired off one or two of his uncoordinated punches, and dropped his arms again. The Goat even managed to read, "You have no idea the things—" Whatever things he was talking about, it was obvious they had to be better than the way Mirco imitated them.

Within a few weeks, the Goat had managed to reconstruct everything. He knew that Mirco had been talking about the day he had seen me training. That name, "the Dancer", had started appearing more and more frequently on the lips of the people around him—like words you don't know that suddenly start cropping up everywhere—to finally reveal the figure of this legendary boxer, who danced in the ring like a butterfly, as fast as a gun and as powerful as a missile. The final shock came when the Goat read on the lips of a guy named Lotti that the Dancer was the same weight as him. He had only to glimpse that handful of syllables, junior welterweight, to understand they were talking about his weight.

That was when the Goat started to become obsessed with my legend. Let's be clear about this, for him there was no one better to play that role: I obviously had an extraordinary talent but I didn't fight, I packed quite a wallop but had a totally inappropriate body, and outside the gym I was the biggest nerd imaginable, as well as being shy and not talking much. In other words, I was a shadow. There were boys at school who boasted about how they'd met me several times and had actually seen me fighting an illegal match in some seedy basement. One day I told one of my fellow singers in the school choir—another thing my mother had forced me to do— that I was a boxing fan. He looked at me with a glint in his eyes and asked me if I had seen Mike Tyson's last fight. Of course, I said, but Tyson is a has-been these days. We talked about boxing for a while and although he made out he was a real connoisseur he didn't know anything. He was convinced that Cassius Clay was Muhammad Ali's constant challenger, and had once even beaten him. It was an interesting mistake, and in its way quite acute, even if unwittingly, but it spoke volumes about his knowledge of sports.

Anyway, after a while he asked me if I had ever heard of the Dancer. I burst out laughing.

"Why are you laughing?"

"No, nothing, forget it."

"Well?"

"Well what?"

"Have you ever heard of him?"

"Yes, a few times."

His eyes lit up again. "Really?"

"Yes, a few times."

"And have you seen him training?"

"No, never."

"I have."

"Oh, sure you have."

"You know he doesn't fight, don't you?"

"Yes, so I heard."

"Or at least not legally."

"Obviously not."

"He says he doesn't fight because when he's in the ring there's a risk he'll kill his opponent."

"Is that right?"

"I swear. My brother trains with him."

"Oh, yes? And what's your brother's name?"

"Enrico."

The only Enrico I knew around the gym was the caretaker, who had three fingers of his right hand missing, and it was as unlikely that he was his brother as that he had ever trained with me.

"What's he look like?"

"Who, my brother?"

"No, the Dancer."

"Oh, he's tall and thin with a small head." So far, the description was spot on. "And he's covered in tattoos and has a long scar over his right eye."

Here it came.

"Imagine that," I said. "I was told he was a very ordinary guy you wouldn't look twice at."

He looked at me and moved his hand up and down, as if to say, "Come on!"

I have no idea who that tone-deaf boy who sang with me in the choir had seen training, or if he had even seen anyone training, or if he even had a brother at all. But it's a good indication of the kind of things people said about me.

And this legend had been started by people who had all their five senses; people who should, with those five senses, have been able to put together a picture that had some connection with reality. But think now about a deaf person, think about someone who, in order to put together that same picture, is forced to gather bits and pieces here and there, wherever he finds them. What are you left with then? You're left with that bloody name that jumps from mouth to mouth and bounces around your head like a stone, always preceded and followed by knowing and admiring looks, until you're going out of your mind.

And when you're a boxer, and you believe in it, and you're good—maybe the best—and you discover that name belongs to someone who weighs the same as you do, then you wait a while and when you can't stand it any more you go to your trainer's office and inform him that you want to fight that name, because the reason you go to that damn gym every bloody day and sweat and slog away like an animal is that you want to be able to say that life isn't shit after all, and you don't really want to be wasting your time because of some little arsehole people call the Dancer.

So it was that the Goat went into Buio's office that day and tossed that piece of paper on his desk with that message— that he wanted to fight me. And Buio, after asking himself why and answering his own question, after wondering how he had found out about the Dancer and telling himself it really didn't matter, looked the boy straight in the eyes for a few seconds, then said, "The Dancer doesn't fight."

The Goat also looked Buio in the eyes for a couple of seconds, then grabbed a pen and a piece of paper, scribbled something on it and tossed it back on Buio's desk.

There was one word on it: *Bullshit.*

"It's not bullshit," Buio said. "I'm telling you the truth, son. The Dancer doesn't fight. I know his trainer Gustavo well. He was my trainer once upon a time. I've seen this guy training many times, and no one really knows why, but he doesn't fight. Even Gustavo splutters when I ask him, and Gustavo isn't the kind of man to splutter. Forget it, son. He's good, yes, but in my opinion you're even better, and anyway, a boxer who doesn't fight, well, it's hardly surprising they call him the Dancer."

The Goat had stopped watching his lips and had started looking him in the eyes again, then he leant over the table, quite calmly wrote something on a little piece of paper, turned and walked out.

Buio picked up the paper, turned it and held it between the thumb and forefinger of both hands, without lifting his arms from the desk. This time, the Goat had written: *Until I fight the Dancer I'm not fighting anyone else.*

No one thought the Goat would carry out his threat, but in fact he missed a regional championship, two friendly matches between gyms, two inter-regional meetings and even the Italian championship, which he probably would have won hands down.

He still trained as enthusiastically as ever, just as if he was going to fight, but whenever Buio took him a form to sign for a match, he would shake his head and quickly go back to whatever it was he was doing.

The first time this happened, Buio phoned Gustavo.

"Hello?"

"Hi, Gustavo, it's Buio."

"Hi, Buio, how's it going?"

"So-so, and you?"

"Feeling old."

"You were saying that thirty years ago."

"But I probably won't be saying it in another thirty years."

Buio gave a little laugh. "Maybe not," he said.

Silence.

"Listen, Gustavo, my boy Mugnaini says until he's fought the Dancer he's not going to fight anyone else. He's already missed an international."

"The one in Lucca?"

"Yes, the one in Lucca. Why weren't you there?"

"Because I didn't have anyone ready."

"OK, but are you going to put the Dancer in a fight or not?"

"No."

"Why not?"

"That's the way it is. It's not up to me."

"How about a little fight between gyms, two rounds, just for fun, to keep my boy happy and get him fighting again? Look, this guy's going to get me to the European championships."

"The Dancer doesn't fight."

"Not at all?"

"Not at all."

"All right, let's keep our fingers crossed."

"How's your wife?"

"Better, thanks. How's yours, still dead?"

"Fuck off, Buio."

The second time, after the friendlies and the Italian championship, Buio came to the gym in person. I wasn't there. I found out by chance the following day from a middleweight named Franco, a not very talented fighter, completely crazy but friendly. He told me that late in the day, as he was on his way out, he had seen Buio go into Gustavo's office and close the door behind him. He also said he thought the reason for his visit was to ask Gustavo to let me fight. As he said this, he looked really moved, like a little boy who was talking about God knows what. The fact is, I heard this story about a fight another couple of times over the next few days.

This was it, the moment had come. I had to get in that fucking ring and demonstrate once and for all that I really was the best, that it wasn't only a fantasy, that I wasn't just a legend, but a person of flesh and blood, muscles and speed. I had to thrash the living daylights out of that deaf mute from the world outside. It would be a bit like thrashing Beethoven, Signora Poli, mother, every other boxer and the whole world—and then once and for all everyone would know that there was a piece of reality, square in shape with ropes all around, where I really was a sensation.

So a few days later I went into Gustavo's office and said, "I want to fight."

Gustavo took his head in his hands and said in that whiny black jazzman's voice of his, like a chugging tractor, "What's got into both of you? You can't fight. Your mother would tear my head off. The last time you went home with a black eye, she came here and threatened to kill my family. Your mother's crazy, son, and I don't want to have anything to do with her. Why are you both so keen to fight anyway?"

"Because we want to know who's the best."

"What do you care? You'll never be in the ring together, because you'll never compete."

"We'll fight, it's the same thing."

"No, it's not the same thing. Drop it, forget that guy, I mean it. It wouldn't be a good fight."

"It would be the fight-of-the-century."

That was it. I'd gone and touched Gustavo's weak point, the weak point of any genuine lover of boxing: the possibility of witnessing a great fight. And even though we both knew it wouldn't be the match-of-the-century, or even of the decade, it was also obvious that it would be a great fight and that everyone was itching to know which of these two great young boxers would get the better of the other. Where he would land a great left I would land a great right, where he would deliver a great uppercut I would deliver a great straight punch, and where he would close up like a goat I would start dancing.

No doubt about it, it would be a great fight.

"Forget it," Gustavo said.

I don't know what happened, but a few weeks later Gustavo called me to his office. Buio was there, sitting on a chair. He stood up and shook my hand, looking almost moved.

"Hello," I said.

Gustavo told me to sit down. He passed his hand over his face and took a deep breath. "So," he said. "You really want this fight?"

I felt every muscle in my face relax. My moment had come. "Yes," I said.

"Then let's do it," Gustavo said. "But no fucking around"— he pointed at both Buio and me—"no sissy little two-round affair. You want to fight? All right. Let's go the full seven rounds. I don't want a fistfight, I want a boxing match, and I want to do it properly. We'll hold it in three months' time, on the twenty-eighth of February at nine in the evening, in your gym, Buio, because you have an Olympic ring, and I'll leave it to you to organise it. We're the beginners, so we'll be the challengers. We'll choose the referee together. I was thinking of Paoli but we'll see. If one of you turns out to be over the weight, the match will be decided by adjudication. If there are any delays due to unforeseen circumstances, accidents and so on, we'll get together and decide what to do, though I can't guarantee we'll keep the challenge going. And you," he said, pointing at me, "if your mother comes here again and starts sounding off, I never want to see you again. Is that clear to everyone?"

Buio and I looked at each other like two little boys called to the headmaster's office and nodded.

"Now fuck off before I change my mind," Gustavo said.

Buio and I left the office with our heads down. Once outside, we shook hands.

"Bye, then."

"Bye."

"See you on the twenty-eighth of February."

"OK. Good luck, then."

"Thanks, you too."

T HEY WERE THE LONGEST three months of my life, and they flew by in an instant. Before I knew it, I was suddenly up there in that damned ring, skipping up and down in the corner with a towel round my shoulders, my face smeared with Vaseline and two beads of sweat already stinging my eyes, suddenly aware that it wasn't a game any more.

Gustavo worked me harder in those three months than he ever had before. He insisted I go running every morning before school, do two hours' training every evening before dinner, go to bed at nine, and so on. At the same time I had to keep up with my schoolwork, my piano lessons, my marks and all those other things that kept my mother quiet and gave me some cards to play with, so I could continue my training and be forgiven for the two black eyes I brought home with me during those three months.

Gustavo would breathe down my neck for nearly an hour about speed, flexibility, developing my potential. Then he'd stick me up there in the ring to face whoever was available, whether they were tall or short, good or not so good, fast or slow, closed or open, technical or otherwise. He would stick them in the ring with me and urge them to wallop me as hard as they could, then from time to time he would stop the clock, get in the ring, give me a couple of slaps on my helmet and show me this or that punch, the mistake I had just made, the uppercut that had turned out so unbalanced … And then he'd give me another slap on my helmet.

"What are you doing? Can you tell me that? You do a dumb bend to your left and fire off an uppercut to the liver without even being properly supported on your legs. Don't you know who it is you're going to fight? Haven't you seen how that boy fights? He's a sniper. That's what he's waiting for—for you to take a big step and lose your balance or leave yourself exposed—and then he'll get in there with one of his killer punches. And remember this, son, he won't wait the way he waited with that nobody from Rome, he won't stand there looking at you, he knows you won't get caught like a sucker that way, he knows you'll keep still. And if he doesn't know it Buio does, he knows I'll stop you and he's seen you train. No, I'll bet my arse he won't wait. From the first round he'll be there in front of you like a block of granite and he'll parry you and tease you until you show him a square centimetre he can sink his fists in, and if you show him that, I guarantee you he'll be in there like a shot. That's all he can do. You're too fast, too tall and too technical for him to fight you any other way. That's all he'll do: keep you at a slight distance and try to find a way in. And once he gets in you're fucked, he's too strong for you, you pansy, do you understand? Do you understand?"

He gave me another slap on my helmet and I nodded, cowed.

"So what were you doing, bending in that sloppy way? Do you know the chance you have of landing an uppercut to the Goat's liver? Hmm, do you? Let me tell you: not much, not much at all. But if you want the truth, in my opinion that's how you'll win the fight, if you win."

Gustavo always had that way of contradicting himself without contradicting himself which took you by surprise.

"What?" I muttered behind the gumshield.

"Yes." Gustavo lowered his voice, as if he suddenly wanted to tell me a story. "In my opinion, that's how you'll win, if you're going to win: you'll hurt him where he least expects it. You have to have balls and the patience not to leave yourself open and not risk a sloppy uppercut, as if you'd just thought of it and were giving it a try. He'll do everything he can to stay close to you and you'll do everything you can to stay away from him. He'll be thinking of those lightning straight punches that'll be raining down on him like hail; he'll be thinking of that right hand you keep up against your chin that's as sharp as a cannonball when you let it go. That's what he'll be afraid of, it's what he'll be watching for, what he'll be keeping an eye on. He'll spend his time keeping you close, looking for a way in and keeping an eye on your right. He'll be convinced that the moment he opens up you'll get in there like a rocket with your right. That's what he'll be afraid of. And he'll be so concerned about it, it's very unlikely you'll actually be able to get in there with that right. But damn it, that deaf-mute little bastard doesn't have a thousand eyes; sooner or later he'll have to forget that you have more than just a right; sooner or later he'll leave his cheek or his liver or his chin exposed … That's when you have to get in and surprise him; that's when you have to come out with a great short hook or a strong uppercut and give him the jolt of his life. Sooner or later, too, he'll have to try and get in a good straight right of his own. And that's where I want you; that's where you have to bend forwards to your left and get in an uppercut to his liver that'll break a rib. Understood?"

I nodded again and Gustavo gave me another slap.

"So what was that crap just now? Why the hell do you bend like a dummy and leave yourself open like a sucker? He has to forget you can do those kinds of punches. Listen to me, son, and I want us to be absolutely clear about this: if, on the night, I see you throw a single pointless hook or uppercut, I swear I'll throw in the sponge and stop the fight. If you risk going for the knockout punch when you don't have it, I swear I'll stop the fight. Get this into your head: if you win this fight, you'll win it either narrowly on points or because you have the patience to wait for the right punch."

That was how Gustavo thought. He trained me like a normal boxer of my size: he made me throw one straight punch after another and made me keep to the centre of the ring and give the initiative to my opponent, holding him at a distance and tormenting him with jabs, but he was convinced that the thing that would clinch the fight would most likely be one of those punches no one would expect: a quick, sharp punch from a short distance, with a lot of weight behind it, which would take my opponent by surprise. And that was something he worked on a lot, too. He would direct me in the ring: the rule was that if he suddenly clapped his hands I had to sidestep and deliver a quick combination of two or three punches, then turn and come out again, possibly rounding it off with a nice quick right just to annoy my opponent. When it worked, he would applaud for a few seconds and yell "GOOD!" but when I got it wrong and laid myself open he would throw a towel or a glove on the floor or stamp his foot and swear and curse me in that croaky black man's voice of his.

One week before the fight, he told me we were there now and for the last days I had to take it easy and get some rest. Of course, I still had to go running, but mainly to work off the excess of lactate, and of course I still had to train, but one hour was enough, and then just gymnastics, or at most a couple of easy rounds, just to keep in practice.

I was wound up like a spring. No one could stop me now. I looked at myself in the mirror at the gym and felt as ready as a real champion. There I was, preparing for the championship of the world; I was Mike Tyson, Muhammad Ali, Sugar Ray Robinson and all the others who, over the generations, had ever skipped up and down on a wooden floor and looked into their own eyes in the mirror like gladiators.

Apparently, the betting had gone through the roof. They gave me three-to-one. They said that in the end the Goat's experience would lay me out flat. They said I was a good boxer, but when you got down to it I was a ballerina, and as soon as I found myself up there I'd be shit-scared and start to fire off pointless punches just like that Roman boy I had seen at the Teatro Tenda. There were even those who said I would be beaten in the first round, or that the Goat would get in the ring and, when the bell rang, would walk to the centre with his head down, parry a couple of jabs the way he knew how, then get inside and cover me in a forest of punches so thick that Gustavo would have to use a chainsaw to get me out.

Luckily, there were also those who liked me, who said I was so accurate and fast and technical I could beat anyone; that however good you were, there was no way to get in close to me without leaving yourself open and getting one of my rights straight between the eyes. There were some who said the Goat would never even get close to me; that he would stand there powerless under a hail of jabs, and from out of that hail would emerge one of my power shots that would lay anyone out flat; that it didn't matter that I'd never fought before, because class is class, and it doesn't really matter if you demonstrate it or not: if you have it you have it, and all anyone else can do is acknowledge your superiority.

Then there were the undecided: those who may have been more far-sighted than the others and really had no idea how it would go, those who had seen both of us and didn't let their imaginations run away with them, those who had come to see us both train during those three months; people you saw after the training session chatting away at the back of the gym, some of them smiling and shaking their heads; people who really didn't see how one of these two boys could get the upper hand over the other because they were both so different and at the same time so similar.

But no one had any doubts that it would be a great fight.

A ND NOW SUDDENLY there I was, up there in that ring, skipping about in the corner, holding my gloves up to my chin as if to pray, my eyes closed, the spotlights over my head, and in front of me and all round the ring those rows of seats and those aisles packed full of excited-looking people drinking beer, talking, watching silently, laughing, concentrating or drawing figures in the air. All those people had come there to see us, to see me, to see this ballerina they had heard so much about, this prince of the ring, rarely seen, the stuff of legends—a real master. They had come there to see if it was really worth telling the stories and believing in them or if, once again, as usually happened, reality would destroy the myths, like a father hitting a little boy who tells a lie, a little boy who only lies because he wants to live a different life from the shit around him. They were there to see a battle between dream and reality, between the world as it was and the way we would like it to be. Or perhaps they only wanted to see once and for all if it's talent or effort that wins out, or whether talent even exists or is just a lot of hot air. There was a whole world hanging over that ring and as the referee walked into the centre of it and the people fell silent I knew that, if I lost, my life would no longer be the same. Maybe if I won, too, but that wasn't what worried me.

I suddenly felt a slap on the face. Gustavo was looking hard at me.

"This is it, son," he said, taking the towel from my shoulders. "Do what you know and don't think about it."

I turned, and there in the centre of the ring were the Goat and the referee, waiting for me. I walked into the

46

centre, skipping and loosening up my arms, until I was in front of him and caught a glimpse of his eyes under the wall he had instead of a forehead. I had never seen him so close. There were already two expressive lines on his cheeks, the muscles were moulded to his body like tight-fitting rubber, his neck fell thick under his ears, and his back and chest were like two marble slabs. He already looked like a man. You didn't get the feeling he was deaf, you got the feeling he was a fighting animal in miniature. You only had to set eyes on him to know he was a boxer, and one of the best. While the referee was speaking, he never took his eyes off a point somewhere at the height of my breastbone, and when, at the referee's request, I touched gloves with him, all he did was turn and go back to his corner, where he started skipping and hitting his own chin just as I had seen him do against the Roman at the Teatro Tenda.

Oh, God, who was I trying to kid? This guy was a real boxer, the kind that actually fights. Not like me, hiding myself away in a gym, persuading myself and other people that I was a sensation, when there's someone outside who's really sweating for that title, with fists and blood. Who did I think I was?

Then the bell went and I found myself in the centre of the ring. The Goat and I touched gloves, and for the first time we looked each other in the eyes. Everything fell into place; my left arm was in front of my eyes and my right arm against my cheek; my legs started to dance around and I started to shower him with straight punches, one after the other, the way you were meant to. It just happened, automatically. We touched gloves, my heartbeat slowed and the sounds of the voices and the cries all around me started fading; there was only me and this half-man in front of me with his head down and his guard up, just like a goat. I showered him with straight punches and he parried them one after the other, or brushed them away with his hand. Every now and again he would bend to one side and attempt a hook or an uppercut, but not very convincingly, as if measuring the distance.

My legs bounced on that green canvas as if they were springs. I skipped, turned and fired off some rather unconvincing straight lefts and rights. I saw the Goat dodge me and launch a few punches without ever taking his eyes off me; those two little black holes that seemed to be joined to my pupils with fishing line.

It occurred to me that it was the same for both of us up there: he'd never heard anything in his life and I'd suddenly become deaf. I actually wondered if, by some magic, he started to hear something when the bell went— if not the voice and the cries, then a few muffled sounds like his own heartbeat, the way I did. I realised suddenly that we were the same breed: both outcasts, both uncool, two boys who were fighting for their lives, for that dirty, square fragment of reality where things happened the way they were supposed to and everything fell into place. And suddenly part of me understood that neither of us could win, that both of us could only lose.

The match continued like that, nice, quiet and clean, for nearly three rounds. I kept my distance and fired off straight punches and as soon as I saw a chink I got in a few warning shots. A couple of times I immediately launched another right, just to show I wasn't playing the fool, to make sure the Goat didn't forget it. I skipped and danced around with my guard held high, keeping to the centre of the ring, trying from time to time to get the Goat into the corner with two punches and get out again before I got stuck there. Everything was too loose, and I had the unpleasant feeling the little deaf bastard was laughing beneath that marble forehead which hung heavily over his eyes; waiting and waiting with the patience of a Tibetan monk for me to make a mistake or get tired. But he never did anything, he just watched me dance, move round the ring and skip in front of him without ever taking his eyes off me, like a machine, just springing lightly on his toes, dodging my straight jabs by a millimetre, and every now and again firing off an uppercut or a couple of small punches. Just once, maybe twice, he did a bit more: I felt two gloves land on me more strongly and determinedly, pinning my elbow to my ribs, followed by a fairly strong hook to make me drop my guard. They were punches just like the others, but stronger, and they seemed to be there simply to say, "Watch out, girl, you can dance round this fucking ring as much as you like, but sooner or later you're going to falter one way or another and then we'll come visiting. That was just a taster."

And at the end of the third round it happened. There I was, skipping and firing off lefts, when suddenly, just as a right set off from my cheek like an elastic band, I saw the little man dodge to the side and felt three punches as hard as stone hit me first in the stomach then on the chin, three punches as solid as bricks that had come from God knows where, landed on my body and slammed me hard against the ropes. I didn't see anything more until suddenly the referee was there in front of me with his Dali moustache, raising the finger in front of my face and moving his mouth like a cartoon character; my hands were clutching the ropes and trying to keep me on my feet, Gustavo was somewhere to the side trying to tell me something, the Goat was in his corner skipping about with his guard up, looking at me from under his forehead like a hit man, and the audience were clapping and yelling. I saw one of the referee's hands fill with fingers, then, slowly, the other one. I hauled myself back on my feet and nodded several times. There are those who claim they heard me say, "Here I am," but I don't remember that. The referee stopped counting, put his hands down, took my gloves, cleaned them on his shirtfront and said something. I kept nodding and trying to say yes, hoping it was enough. After barely a moment, the referee walked away and called the Goat back into the centre of the ring. He looked twenty centimetres taller and ten kilos heavier, his muscles were bulging and he seemed to be coming towards me like an avalanche. I would have liked to be in a cartoon film, rolling my eyes and running away in a puff of smoke, but I couldn't, I wasn't even sure I could move. All I could do was close myself up behind my gloves, lean on the ropes, wait for the avalanche to arrive, and hope it wouldn't be too violent and that it wasn't long till the end of the round. The avalanche arrived in a shower of uppercuts to the body, first a series of six or seven as fast as a machine gun, then some slower but stronger ones, one after the other, like tree trunks falling on me from a height of twenty metres. They landed like anvils, many of them on my elbows, and their purpose didn't seem to be to bring me down, but to make something clear: they didn't have the speed, precision and unpredictability of a knockout blow, but the rhythm and power of a lesson. "So far we've been playing," they said. "It's time for the big boys now." And, yes, luckily the round was soon over.

But it didn't really matter. That little man in miniature knew perfectly well when exactly to send me off, he had waited for that moment just so that he could send me back to my corner with the impact of those punches still on my ribs; with my head spinning and the knowledge that the games as I'd known them were over and now we were starting to fight.

I was an idiot: for three rounds, just like that Roman kid, I had played his game; I had tired myself out thinking he would never find a way in, throwing punches that were as clean and accurate as you could wish, just not very effective. And even though I hadn't panicked like the Roman, I'd been an idiot and taken things too casually, and the Goat had punished me for it.

But to be honest, that wasn't the tragedy, nor was it the fact that I'd suddenly realised what a boxing match was, what a real boxer was and what it meant to really fight. It wasn't the certainty that my life had suddenly changed. And it wasn't the feeling that things were slipping through my fingers and I was losing. No, the real tragedy was that in an instant the spell had been broken. In an instant, after that series of punches which had pinned me to the ropes, the noise of the shouting and all the rest had come rushing back like a goods train, and I didn't see the punches coming in slow motion any more: I'd lost the almost magical feeling that allowed me to play with my opponents, that kind of slowed-down vision that let me see the punches, not before they were launched but while they were still in motion, and act accordingly. Suddenly, reality had put itself back together in front of my eyes just as it was, at its own speed, and that terrified me.

Gustavo slapped me a few times and asked if I was all right. He told me later that I kept saying, "Everything's normal, everything's normal." He wasn't sure everything was normal, and the fact that I kept repeating it certainly didn't convince him, but he decided that if everything was normal for me then, when you got down to it, it had to be normal for him, too.

If I had to choose the worst time of my life, if I had to isolate one time in my existence and give it the stupid label of the worst time of all, I'd give it to those six or seven minutes up there in that ring, those fourth and fifth rounds. The Goat was no longer that deaf boy with the forehead like a wall and the dark eyes who liked to box, the Goat was suddenly Life itself, which had taken me outside that world of playthings where I was a sensation who could see punches coming in slow motion, and in the form of that boy had started hitting me so often I wanted to beg for mercy. I skipped round the ring, risked a few straight punches, and that knot of muscle followed me like a mad dog, bending and hitting me with punches as heavy as wood, in the liver, in the ribs, on the chin, or on the gloves or the shoulders when he missed. He would be there in front of me, panting, then he would take half-a-step to the side and fire off an explosive series of three punches that would have knocked down a door—luckily not all that accurate most times, and luckily that part of me that was still playing the role of a boxer managed not to lay itself open to that surge of anger.

Two rounds, and a lesson to last a lifetime. But he got things wrong, too, and by the sixth round he was tired. His fists had rained down on me, and yet I was still there somehow, skipping in front of him—I hadn't gone down, and I had demonstrated, whether I had the body for it or not, whether I had a neck like a chicken or not, that I was capable of staying on my feet.

There are some who claim it was the best fight they ever saw in their lives. I don't know about that, I somehow doubt it, but if ever I suspect it might be true, it's because of those last two rounds. I had strutted like a rooster for three rounds, he had punished me for another two, and now he was tired and I had come back to reality, and suddenly we looked at each other from the centre of the ring like two boxers, sweaty, stinking, scared, tired, angry, ready to lose and to give our all to win. We both realised it, because we touched gloves again. We found ourselves in the centre of the ring, me skipping and him looking straight at me after another of his three-punch combinations: we looked each other in the eyes for a moment, and I'm sure that even though our lips didn't move, we both smiled, put out our hands and slammed our gloves together. The voices and shouts around us vanished again, but the punches didn't start coming in slow motion again, they came just as they were launched, strongly and accurately. I started doing again what I knew best, but like anyone else now, working hard: one straight punch after the other. Left, left, parry, turn, turn, left right left. He would be in front of me, moving his head from side to side, waiting for me to launch another wave of punches; he would come in from underneath and fire off two punches as hard as wood; as he moved away I would land two more straight punches, without even breathing, hoping to recover my strength from somewhere, hoping that those two lead poles attached to my shoulders continued to do their job and didn't leave me standing there like a burst tyre. Punch, parry, punch, straight, straight, left-right, take it, take it, take it, parry, step back, straight punch.

The audience were on their feet, and when the bell rang for the end of the sixth round and we went back to our corners for the last time, they applauded in a composed way, as if they were at the theatre. I like to think my mother was there, too, somewhere at the back of the hall, and that she started crying.

Gustavo kept saying, "You're a sensation, you're a sensation. Come on, it's the last round. You're a sensation, son, just one more round." I wasn't listening, I was looking at those people clapping and when Gustavo's back moved out of the way, I peered at him in the other corner, Mugnaini the Goat, and wondered if I would ever again in my life share something as big as this with another person.

The referee ordered the seconds out, the bell rang one last time, and we went back into the centre of the ring to touch gloves again. And we started again, going for broke, doing what we were there to do, me firing off my straight punches and dancing and him coming towards me head down and pounding away. I took a couple of nasty lefts to the stomach and he caught a few worrying lefts and a strong straight right to the chin, which for a moment almost made him stagger. We didn't give each other time to breathe, it was one punch after another, parry, right, left, right, left, left, parry, parry, bull's eye, step back, left right. Our arms were as heavy as anchors and our legs were like logs newly planted in the earth. I had stopped dancing, I was walking round the ring firing off straight punches as best I could and trying to keep my guard up and parry whenever he came towards me.

Giano taped the fight. I must have watched it five hundred times, and every time I wonder if that thin boy up there who looks as if he's fighting for his life is really me. I wonder if I still have that courage, or if I fritter it away every day minute by minute, or if I've lost it, scattered it somewhere among the bricks of my house or in the fat around my waist or in my mother's grave.

But Gustavo was right, the Goat fell into the trap of wanting too much. It had been a great fight, and we were in the hands of the judges now. I had understood that, but he hadn't, he wanted the killer punch, he wanted to guarantee the result for himself and make it clear once and for all which of us really was the stronger of the two: he tried to get me where I least expected it, with a long, fast straight right to the chin. And I have to be honest: a few rounds earlier I might have been rattled, I might not even have expected that straight thunderbolt to the chin, as fast as a train. But not at that point, not a few seconds from the end; not now when it really didn't matter if I was expecting something or not, because I was protecting myself from everything; not now when he was slower than he thought, and predictable. I almost saw him launch that right, and I'd like to be able to say I was quick-witted enough to pivot on my foot and land the decisive combination, but, although that was exactly what I did, it happened purely by automatic reflex, as if someone else was giving the orders. I don't know, maybe that's what talent is: something that's out of our hands, something we're slaves of, whether we like it or not.

The Goat waited for two of my lefts, parried to the side, delivered a left uppercut to my liver, took a small step back and fired off that textbook straight right with the full force of his arm. I moved my right leg, pivoted on my left foot and sent a sharp left uppercut straight to the Goat's chin, under his arm, followed immediately by a right hook that sent the Goat flying back against the ropes. I wish I hadn't then launched that final straight punch, I really wish I hadn't, but it came just like that, by itself. If I could turn the clock back, I would stop myself firing off that final thunderbolt, I really would stop myself, I wouldn't let one stupid punch determine the future of two people forever. I would let that right hook run its course and watch the boy bounce against the ropes, would make it clear it was a mistake, then take two steps back and let the last few seconds run on in all their glory. But when you're there you don't have much choice, and anyway there are moments when you can't really control what happens to you. So I landed that right hook and then, just as the Goat slammed into the ropes, a missile was launched from somewhere near my face and hit my opponent's chin like a thunderbolt, flinging him from the ropes and laying him out on the canvas a metre from me.

The referee pushed me away and sent me to my corner, then started counting. He had just counted six when the bell went. Gustavo had decided with Buio that if the bell went when a fighter was down, he'd be saved by it. I don't know why, maybe that's the kind of decision no one ever knows how to make, and in the end you decide by tossing a coin. Heads you're saved by the bell, tails you aren't. That time, if that was really what had happened, heads had won. That's life, we say, and we think we're in control of everything.

But in the end it didn't really matter what the rules said. We both knew how the fight had gone. The Goat knew it and I knew it and Gustavo knew it and Buio and anyone in that packed gym who knew anything about boxing. The bell rang and after a few seconds Mugnaini was picked up and carried to his corner; his gloves were slowly taken off, he was given smelling salts and presumably Buio told him that he had been saved by the bell, but that that was fine, because it had been a great fight, one of the best he had ever seen.

In my corner, Gustavo massaged my shoulders, hugged me, congratulated me and told me again that I was a sensation, and that I had won all the fights I wanted to that night. I didn't understand. Suddenly, it was over. I had done it; I had finished the fight and had stayed on my feet and if it hadn't been for the bell I might even have won. And now I felt empty and alone; I had the rest of my life in front of me and all of a sudden I had to figure out what to do with it.

The trainers put our towels round us and made us get up, turn to the audience and wave. The audience stood up with us, clapping, whistling and yelling incomprehensibly.

The referee said the judges were about to deliver their ruling and called us both into the centre of the ring. The Goat came forwards with his head down, massaging his neck. He looked like a frightened little boy, nothing like the raging avalanche that had attacked me not so long before. Even his eyes seemed clearer, his forehead less massive. I wondered how I looked. Actually if I look at the photos I don't seem all that different, just tired, and perhaps a little bewildered.

We stood on either side of the referee, he took our hands and we waited for the judges to deliver their ruling. We stood there, our sweat glistening under the spotlights, the audience suddenly silent but all on their feet, waiting and staring at us as if we were heroes. It was just like a fight on TV. If I continued, would my nickname always be the Dancer, I wondered, and would his always be the Goat, or was that kind of thing only for young boys?

From somewhere came a voice that bounced around the walls: "BY A UNANIMOUS DECISION, THE JUDGES DECLARE THAT THE MATCH HAS BEEN WON BY BOTH CONTESTANTS EQUALLY."

The hall exploded, the way it does after any controversial fight. There were some who applauded, raised their hands and cried "BRAVO!", others who threw pieces of paper and cried "THIEVES!" and others "IT'S A FIX!" Some people laughed and shook their heads, some nodded, pleased with the outcome, and some went over some of the punches, already getting ready to tell their friends who weren't there all about the fight, trying to find the most vivid words to describe it.

The referee raised our arms, and the Goat, being short, hung there in a kind of lopsided way. Then he let them drop and shook our hands and congratulated us.

The Goat and I found ourselves face to face. I like to think that, like that smile through our teeth in the sixth round, this, too, was a moment that no one noticed. Suddenly here we were, close to each other without our gloves on, both winners, both losers. Our weapons were gone, and we both had to come to grips with what remained of our lives. We hugged briefly in the centre of the ring and felt the touch of each other's naked, sweaty bodies. He muttered a thank you, I said thank *you*. And I don't know if either us knew what we were saying thank you for.

WITH THE FIGHT OVER, everything carried on much the same as before: I would get up, go to school, study, get good marks. Everything, though, was different somehow. Overnight, everything had become real. Perhaps that's what growing up means: realising how things really are. If you think about it, it's as fascinating as it is sad, and although you know you couldn't live any other way there's also a touch of melancholy in admitting it.

I even started to like the piano. Overnight, I realised it was another thing I was good at, whether I liked it or not, and I had the feeling that somehow even that deaf bastard Beethoven was coming back to life in my hands. Above all, I realised how great the music was.

Yes, I also continued training, but even that was different. Now I was really the best, the strongest, there was no doubt about it now—but I was strong like any other boxer, like any other man. Not with the unreal, artificial strength of a legend, but with the stinking, sweaty strength of a man. It was the same outside: now I was just a nerd who couldn't live the way you were supposed to, I wasn't some mysterious comic book character, I wasn't a Peter Parker or Clark Kent ready to save the world with his fists of steel. Now I was just one person among many who wasn't invited to parties, who didn't have a moped and couldn't stay out later than midnight, and it didn't really matter if there was a piece of the world, square in shape and with ropes round it, where I'd fought with the Goat; that didn't change the clothes on my back and didn't sort out my life.

One day, three or four months after the fight, I got an envelope in the post with a medal inside. On the medal were the words *G Cotti Boxing Tournament—First Prize Junior Welterweight*.

I had no idea who G Cotti was. I went to the gym and showed the medal to Gustavo. He took it in his hand from behind the scuffed brown Formica desk and turned it over in his fingers.

"The G Cotti is a meeting that's held once a year near Bologna," he said. Then he looked at me for a few seconds. "Don't you know who won this year?"

"No," I said.

Gustavo lifted the phone and dialled a number, then waited a few seconds, still turning the medal over in his hand.

"Hello," he said. " … Hi, Paolino, it's Gustavo. Yes, fine, fine. And you? … Oh, good, I'm glad to hear it … Well, what can you do, that's how it is. Listen … Yes, yes, quite a bit. Listen … Well, you know how it is. Listen … No, nothing, I just wanted to know if you went to the Cotti … Just curiosity. I didn't have anyone to take, so I … Oh, good, congratulations … Yes … Yes … "

Gustavo looked down at the medal and turned it over in his hand.

"Yes, listen, did you have anyone in the junior welterweight … ? Oh, you didn't? But do you happen to know who won?"

Gustavo looked up and stared at me for a couple of seconds, nodding.

"Oh, right, in the second round. Great fight, eh? … That's fine, thanks a lot, Paolino, see you soon … Sure, you too, thanks. Bye."

Gustavo put down the telephone, tossed the medal on the desk, then looked at me.

"It's the Goat's, he won the Cotti. Knockout in the second round. Paolino says he got up in the ring and the other poor bastard didn't even have time to draw breath. He says it was amazing he managed to stand until the second round. The Goat won by default."

"So how come I have this medal?"

Gustavo suddenly seemed shorter than usual, or maybe I seemed taller. "I don't know, son, I have no idea," Gustavo said, shaking his head slightly, the sides of his mouth turned down pensively. Then for a few seconds he stared at the medal. To tell the truth, he did seem to have some idea, but pretended he didn't.

It was a gift, I thought. It was a tribute or a symbol, I thought. I thought a whole load of things. But then I decided it didn't matter; whatever the Goat meant by that gesture, there was no point spoiling it with words.

A few weeks later, though, I received another envelope with another medal in it. This one bore the words *Italian Championships First Heats—First Prize Junior Welterweight.*

The next day I went to Buio's gym. When I walked in, everyone slowed down or stopped training, and some people leant towards their neighbours to say something. I felt like Rocky going back to the Apollo gym after years away. I asked a boy who was at the punchbag where Buio was, and he told me very politely that he was in his office.

"What about Mugnaini?"

"Who?"

"The Goat."

"Sorry, no one's seen him today. He may be in later."

"Thanks."

"Don't mention it."

"Is the office that way?"

"Yes."

"Thanks again."

"Don't mention it, it's a pleasure."

I could already hear the rumours that would circulate about this visit. I saw them pass in front of my eyes like newspaper headlines: '*THE BALLERINA ISSUES A NEW CHALLENGE*'; '*FIXED MATCH: UNFINISHED BUSINESS*'; '*TWO JUDGES INVESTIGATED FOR FRAUD*'; '*THE BALLERINA DEMANDS JUSTICE*'.

Buio's office was a small room at the back of the gym with a cracked frosted-glass door. I walked past the ring, where two boys with helmets on had stopped to watch me. It seemed like only yesterday that I had got up there with my face covered with Vaseline and that chilling feeling inside that I'd passed the point of no return. I felt like a soldier returning ten years later to a battlefield. Ten years. That much time had passed since that boy had got up in the ring, a boy who still believed in stories and was convinced he had superpowers, could see the world at a different speed and didn't sweat, who thought that everything was easy and that there was a place free from the normal laws of the world and nature. That much time had passed since the death of that boy who hated the piano and everything around him and still believed that stories and reality could be made from the same material. There wasn't much more hair on my face that day in the gym than there had been last time, when I had come in here to conquer the ring, and yet my steps had a quite different rhythm, they already had that heavier, shuffling rhythm of a half-man which would be with me for the rest of my life.

Suddenly, Buio threw open the door of his office and came out yelling, "WHY'S IT SO QUIET OUT HERE, YOU LOSERS? ARE WE TRAINING OR NOT? DO I ALWAYS HAVE TO BE HERE?"

Then he saw me and abruptly calmed down.

"Hello," he said.

"Hello." I shook his hand. "I'd like to talk to you."

"Of course, my pleasure. Franco, go on, get out, we'll talk later."

A sweaty boy in grey trunks got up and went out, nodding slightly to me as he did so.

"CARRY ON TRAINING, YOU LOT!" Buio screamed, closing the door. Then he turned, squeezed my shoulder and smiled. "It's so good to see you. How are you?"

"Not bad, thanks, not bad at all."

"Still training?"

"Yes, still training."

"I'm pleased to hear it. It'd be a pity if you weren't. Can I offer you something?"

"No, I'm fine, thanks."

We were like two Thirties gangsters; all we needed were the raincoats and the felt hats.

"Listen," I said, and I dug the Cotti medal out of my pocket and showed it to Buio. "This came for me a while ago."

Buio took it from me, sat down, sighing, and leant forwards with his elbows on the desk.

"I think it's the Goat's," I went on.

"I know, it was thanks to me he won it. He didn't even want to go to that meeting, he said it would be a waste of time. He was probably right."

"Well, anyway, I got another one yesterday from the first heats of the Italian championships."

"That one, too?"

"That one, too."

I tossed the second medal on the table.

Buio stared at me and sank back into his armchair.

I didn't know what to make of that stare, but there seemed to be a lot of thoughts going through his mind.

We were both silent for a while. Buio kept staring at those medals and turning them over in his hands. From time to time he looked up and gave me a quick glance.

"Do you know where the Goat lives?" I asked at last.

Buio looked at me with raised eyebrows. "Why?"

"What do you mean, why? Because these medals aren't mine, they're his, he won them. I don't want them."

Buio looked at me for a few seconds. "Son," he said, "the Goat doesn't want these medals back, so there's no point embarrassing him. He knows as well as we all do that you won that fight. You're the best, that's what he's trying to say to you, and there's nothing you can do. You're both good fighters, but you're better than he is, and you demonstrated it up there in that ring, with your fists. So stop thinking and just enjoy it."

When I left I decided to go home on foot. I was a little puzzled. I had the feeling this was man's business, and I wasn't used to it.

HORSES

ONE DAY, their father tapped lightly on the doorpost and came in. They didn't know what to think at first: their dad never came to their room unless there was something important he wanted to talk about—usually a problem.

Natan's hand froze in mid-air as he polished his boots; Daniel jerked his head up and cursed to himself. It was sure to be bad news: most likely the old lady at the end of the road had been complaining to their father again, to say they had been stealing drinks from her cellar. The boys loved the old woman's drinks, and not only because when they drank they felt as if everything was rolling downwards, but also and especially because they made them feel more adult. The fact that the drinks were stolen just added to the pleasure.

"Come outside," their father said.

Natan and Daniel looked at each other, a look full of many unspoken feelings that darted in and out of their thoughts like carts going downhill. Natan was the best cart driver in the area. Daniel had only beaten him a couple of times over the years, and one of those was because a wheel had come off Natan's cart.

The two boys were almost shaking as they left the room. It was like a slap in the face, reminding them they were only young. They filed like prisoners through the big kitchen and the living room to the front door. Their father calmly walked ahead of them, not saying a word, not turning round once. He was like a Greek statue in motion, with the same rigid, still perfection.

Outside, the sun was playing a strange early spring game with a couple of clouds, and the wind raced through the tall pines round the farmyard. Over the years, Natan would come to miss that farmyard and those giant pines.

There were two horses tied to the fence, a bay and a chestnut. Their long necks were bent towards the ground and, as the boys and their father started crossing the gravel, the horses turned their big heads. The boys' father stopped in the middle of the farmyard and the two boys came level with him.

"They're for you," he said. There was no warmth in the words; they seemed to come from some cold valley in the north.

The two boys looked at their father. They did not know what to say. They all stood there for a while, staring at the animals.

"Dad, we never asked for horses," Natan said. Daniel envied his brother's courage. He would always envy his brother's courage, just as his brother would always envy his will-power.

"Well, now you have them," their father said. "So you'd better take care of them. I don't have time for any more of your nonsense."

He waited another couple of seconds, then turned and walked back to the house.

"Are they tame?" Daniel called without taking his eyes off the horses, just turning his head slightly to one side.

"Almost," their father replied at the last moment before he went in through the door and was swallowed by the darkness of the interior.

The two boys stood there, side by side, not knowing what to say or do, both feeling suddenly as if there was a dead weight on their backs.

Natan spat on the gravel and moved his tongue over his teeth. "Fuck," he said, twisting his neck slightly to one side.

It's always the same: you don't know what you have until you've lost it. That was what Daniel thought years later, whenever he remembered that moment.

"What now?" Daniel asked, already knowing the answer.

"We don't seem to have much choice," Natan said.

"No, we don't," Daniel said.

Natan spat on the gravel again. "Fuck. Who the hell gives a damn about horses?"

"We'd better start giving a damn about them," Daniel said.

The two boys stood there, side by side, staring at the horses, which to be honest were handsome animals.

"They're not bad," Daniel said.

Natan turned for a moment and looked frostily at his brother, then spat on the gravel again.

"Fuck," he said again. Natan liked to swear, especially when he was nervous.

WHEN OLD PANCIA SAW the two brothers coming down the path, it struck him as funny: he had woken up that day with the feeling that something strange was going to happen. Old Pancia didn't much like feelings, and certainly didn't like paying them any heed—but then they usually turned out to be true, which bothered him even more.

The second thing that struck old Pancia was that the boys had stolen the horses from some nearby farm, but if they had he'd surely have known about it. Old Pancia knew practically every horse in the area; he had tamed them, brought most of them into the world, and those he hadn't weren't worth bothering with. These two horses, though, he'd never seen—there was no way you'd forget two animals like that.

When they reached the enclosure where old Pancia was working, Daniel was the first to speak.

"They say you deal with horses," he said.

Old Pancia was mending the fence with a hammer. "Who says that?" he replied, without looking up from his work.

"People."

"What people?"

"People round here."

"Oh, is that what they say?"

"You *are* old Pancia?"

Old Pancia looked up at them for the first time. "What do you think?"

The two boys looked him up and down for a few seconds. He was a big man, who looked quite a bit older than he was, with a fat, bulging belly that pushed his shirt out of his trousers so that it hung down like a skirt.

"I think you are," Daniel said.

"You're a clever boy," old Pancia said.

Daniel decided not to answer.

"Are they tame?" old Pancia asked.

"Almost."

"What does that mean?"

"We don't know, that's what our father said."

"I know your father," old Pancia said. He had now broken off from mending the enclosure, had pushed his straw hat back from his forehead and had leant with his arms on the fence, just in front of them.

"I'm pleased to hear it," Daniel said.

"They're fine horses," old Pancia said.

The three of them were silent for a few seconds.

Natan shifted his weight from one foot to the other and spat on the ground. "Well?" he said. "Can you see to them or not?"

For a moment, Pancia looked Natan in the eyes. "I don't come cheap," he said.

"We don't have any money," Natan said curtly.

Old Pancia waited another couple of seconds, then said, "Who's going to mount them?"

The two brothers looked at each other, not sure what the old man was talking about.

"Who are they for?" the old man said. "Who's going to be riding them?"

Daniel nodded that he had understood. "We are," he said.

The old man adjusted the straw hat on his head. "Then you should be the ones to take care of them."

"We don't know anything about horses."

"I know what there is to know."

"It's a deal, then," Daniel said.

"Like hell it is," old Pancia said. "I don't come cheap."

"We don't have any money," Natan said again.

"You could work for me."

"We can't work for you. All we want to do is tame these horses and learn to ride them."

"I don't give a fuck what you want. If you can't pay me, work for me. Otherwise, you might as well sell these animals for meat and run away before your father finds out."

Natan lowered his head and spat on the ground again. "Fuck," he said.

"When should we come back?" Daniel asked.

"Tomorrow morning at dawn."

"Shit," Natan said.

"Where do we leave the horses?" Daniel asked.

Old Pancia motioned to them to follow him and moved the horses into two small diagonal spaces inside the stable, in the middle of the other horses. Then he said goodbye to the two boys and told them he'd be waiting for them the following morning.

For three months, the boys went to old Pancia's every morning at dawn, and returned home after nightfall. They cleaned the stables, changed the hay and straw and fed the horses. As time passed, the old man taught them how to behave towards the animals, how to take them out, how to clean them, how to use the currycombs and the brushes, how to saddle them and how to put on the bit and bridle.

After only a few weeks, when the boys were already moving around among the animals as if they had been doing it all their lives and he decided they had already paid off most of their debt, old Pancia took them aside one evening and told them to go and take their horses. For Natan, who was already starting to get bored, it couldn't have come any sooner. But Daniel said nothing. So the old man carried on, teaching them how to get the horses to walk in a circle in the enclosure, how to punish them and how to stroke them. When at last the horses were ready, he gave them the saddles and bridles. The horses shied, reared up on their hind legs and whinnied, their ears pinned back and their eyes inflamed with fear.

But in the end, as usual, old Pancia calmed them down and managed to get the boys, who at times had seemed more scared than the animals, to saddle the two horses. Both boys had learnt to command respect: Daniel through the sweat of his brow, the hours he had spent determinedly working with his bay, and Natan through sheer anger, cursing and kicking like a stevedore.

When at last the two horses were tamed, responding to every command in the enclosure, the old man and the boys stood side by side, admiring their handiwork. It was a late afternoon in summer and all three were sweating, bearing the marks of a long day's work. They were leaning on the fence of the enclosure and, to put it bluntly, each felt a little more of a man.

"What now?" Daniel asked.

"Now you have to learn to ride them."

Natan spat on the ground. "Shit," he said.

Old Pancia laughed and started towards the house. "See you tomorrow at dawn."

I T WAS IMMEDIATELY CLEAR to everyone that the horses would take the two brothers to different places. It's pointless to keep telling ourselves that we are all equal, we all make use of the world in our own way—to get, despite ourselves, to wherever we are meant to be. Some of us use a knife to kill, others to peel an apple. The same knife, but it makes the world different for each one of us.

The villagers soon became accustomed to seeing that figure on horseback wandering on the hill with the sun behind him, and it wasn't long before Natan told his brother that he wanted to go west, beyond the hill, and visit the city. They had heard a lot about the city, even though no one really seemed to know much about it.

"Are you coming, too?" Natan asked his brother.

"No," Daniel said.

They were both sitting on their horses, leaning on their long necks, looking down at the valley. Natan nodded and said nothing.

One morning, Daniel went to a nearby farm: there were two horses there that needed shoeing, and old Pancia had asked him to go. During the months he had spent with old Pancia, Daniel had learnt everything there was to know about horses. Natan, on the other hand, had been content just to learn what he needed.

Although he'd finished taming his bay, Daniel had continued going to old Pancia's. He would give him a hand and pick up some money, which he'd either save or spend on a couple of drinks down at the village inn. He and his brother had stopped stealing drinks from the cellar of the old woman at the end of the road. That was something they missed from time to time, but that's how it was. In the same way, they sometimes missed racing their carts downhill.

When Daniel got to the farm, he saw three men in the stable, standing round a thin, hollow-looking mare, talking. The mare was a fine, tall, solid chestnut, but it was as if some mad sculptor had gone over her from head to foot, chiselling away until there was not much left.

"Hello," Daniel said.

One of the men turned and screwed up his eyes to get a better look at the figure standing against the light. His face was creased and weathered by the sun and his legs bent outwards by overwork, like two bows.

"Hello," the man with the bow legs said.

The other two men looked at Daniel in silence. They were chewing straws.

"I've come to shoe the horses," Daniel said.

One of the two men who were chewing straws gave a half-laugh. He, too, had a weathered face and bow legs.

"Old Pancia must be slipping," the man who had not laughed said.

"That isn't a job for boys," the first man said, standing in front of Daniel.

"If I can't manage, you can complain to old Pancia and he'll come and do it for free."

One of the two men leaning against the stable wall took the straw from his mouth and pushed back his straw hat to get a better look at this boy who talked like a man.

"Come on, then," the first man said with a shrug and started to walk out.

"What's the matter with that mare?" Daniel asked, without moving.

The man who was on his way out stopped and turned to the animal. "She's sick," he said. "She's dying."

"What's wrong with her?" Daniel asked.

"She's old. She's stopped eating and drinking. Must be cancer."

"Can I?" Daniel asked, indicating the mare with his chin.

The man shrugged again and gestured to him to go ahead. Daniel approached the mare and one of the other two men moved away from the stable wall with a smug look on his face, still chewing his straw.

Daniel entered the stable and started to move his hands over the mare's back, legs and stomach. As he went round the front of her to get to the other side, he gave her a couple of slaps on the neck and pulled her upper lip to see her teeth, then moved a hand over her muzzle as if stroking her and walked to the other side.

"She's a fine animal," he said from behind the mare.

The man who had let him go into the stable looked at that heap of bones with the swollen belly and let out a laugh.

"She's old and sick," the first man said, the one who had been about to go with Daniel to shoe the horses. "She's no use to anyone any more."

Daniel came out from behind the animal and, trailing a hand over her back, walked out of the stable. "What are you planning to do with her?" he asked.

"What can we do? We're taking her to the abattoir," the man at the door said.

Daniel turned back to the mare and moved his hand over her again, this time on her hind quarters. "I'll buy her from you," he said after a couple of seconds.

The two men leaning on the fence laughed loudly this time.

The man at the door also burst out laughing. "And how much would you give me?"

"Whatever the abattoir gives you. How much do you think the abattoir will give you?"

The man said a high figure.

Daniel looked him in the eyes for a moment and gave a little laugh. "You'll be lucky to get half that for this bag of bones. You'll be lucky if the abattoir doesn't laugh in your face."

The three men had stopped laughing now. The man at the door, though, was still smiling. "What figure did you have in mind?" he asked, slightly twisting his head round.

"Half that, less something for saving you the trouble of taking her to the abattoir. I'll take her with me today after I've finished shoeing the horses."

The man stopped smiling and thought it over for a few seconds, without taking his eyes off Daniel. "Half exactly, trouble or no trouble."

Daniel turned for a moment to take a last glance at the mare and looked at the man in the doorway again. "It's a deal," he said, and walked up to the man with his hand out.

The man took his hand and shook it. "Deal," he said.

It was the first deal Daniel had done in his life and, as he followed the man out of the stable to go and shoe the other horses, he felt an electric shock down his back and a sensation as if a length of silk were unwinding round his shoulders.

Daniel followed the man who had sold him the mare into a large open space, where three horses were tied to big iron rings in the wall. Daniel walked round to the other side of his bay and started taking tools out of the big bags slung over the horse's back. He placed the tools on the ground, tied a large piece of dark, heavy leather round his waist, picked up the tools again and approached the horses.

"Do you want me to hold the nose clippers for you?" the man asked.

Daniel stopped and turned. "The what?"

"The nose clippers. To keep the horse still."

"Oh, no thanks, there's no need."

The man looked a little puzzled. Daniel had heard that some people, when shoeing horses, used a kind of tongs that squeezed the horse's nose so that the pain made it keep still.

He had talked about it once to old Pancia.

"Rubbish," the old man had replied.

"Isn't it true?"

"Yes, it's true."

"So why's it rubbish?"

"Because you don't need it."

Daniel had said nothing and continued his work.

"Did anyone ever cut your nails?" old Pancia had asked after a while.

Daniel had thought about it. "Of course," he had said.

"And did they use clippers to squeeze your nose and keep you still?"

"What's that got to do with it?"

"I'd like to see how you'd react if, when they cut your nails, they beat your hands with a hammer and filed them with a wooden file. Maybe they'd need nose clippers to keep you still, too."

Daniel had thought about it and in the end had decided that he wouldn't turn a hair.

"So what are you saying?" he had asked finally.

"I'm saying you just have to do it gently," old Pancia had said, and had carried on with his work.

That was why Daniel had never used either nose clippers or any rope or tool to keep a horse still. He would go there and give the animal a couple of slaps, let it smell his smell, give it half a carrot and then try to do the job as gently as possible. Usually by the time he finished whoever was with him would be staring at him, the way children stand and stare for hours at a man carving wooden statuettes.

When Daniel returned, leading the sick mare on a rope, old Pancia was loading a wheelbarrow with fodder.

"What's that one?" the old man asked, leaning on the shovel, when Daniel and the horses came level with him.

"You have to lend me some money," Daniel said as he dismounted.

The old man said nothing, did not move, but just looked at Daniel as if he were an idiot.

"I'll pay you back," Daniel said when he noticed, taking the tool bags off his horse.

"How?"

This time it was Daniel who looked at the old man as if he were stupid. "By working, Pancia."

"What do you need it for?"

Daniel gave the mare's neck a couple of good slaps. "I bought this mare," he said, with a satisfied smile.

Old Pancia looked for a few seconds at Daniel smiling happily, then at that heap of bones that must once have been a horse, and had to make an effort not to burst out laughing. It was only the respect he had for the boy that stopped him.

Instead, he said, "Are you mad?"

Daniel stopped smiling and grew serious again. "Why?"

"What do you mean, 'why'? Can't you see the state she's in?"

Daniel turned, and looked again at his new purchase and moved a hand over her. "In my opinion, she's suffering from the same things as that horse your friend cured for us."

A few months earlier, one of old Pancia's horses had stopped eating and drinking and had grown visibly thinner. It wasn't old and seemed to want to die. No one knew what was wrong with it, until one day a friend of the old man's had turned up with a couple of horses. The old man had taken his friend to see the sick horse. He had walked all round the animal for a few minutes, punching it in the stomach, then he told them to give the horse, by force if need be, a mixture of hot water and some herbs Daniel had never heard of. Within a few days the horse had recovered, but it had been too late to ask the old man's friend what the animal had been suffering from.

The old man rested the shovel against the wheelbarrow and approached the mare with a serious expression on his face. He moved one hand over her nose and the other up and down her front legs, then slapped her on the neck a couple of times and gave her a few punches in the stomach. Finally, he walked round her and came back to where Daniel was standing, without ever taking his hands and eyes off the animal.

"How much do you need?" old Pancia asked.

Daniel gave a slight smile, without Pancia noticing. "Not much."

The old man looked him up and down for a moment, impatiently, then looked at the mare again.

"I've put something aside," Daniel said.

"What if it isn't that?"

"If it isn't that, I'll take her to the abattoir before she dies and get my money back."

The old man was silent for a moment. "And if it is that?"

82

Daniel smiled. "If it is, I got a good deal."

The old man smiled, too. "She's not a bad animal," he said, giving her another couple of slaps on the back.

"I know," Daniel said.

The old man turned and gave him a little smack. "Go inside, and put on some water to boil, and get some of those herbs left over from the other time. We'll see if you got a good deal or not."

In the end, it turned out that Daniel had been right. For a few days the mare had been force-fed the mixture recommended by old Pancia's friend, and suddenly had started eating and drinking as if for two. It took several weeks, though, for her to be back on form. Little by little Daniel helped her to put on weight, then got her moving, trotting round the enclosure. Day after day he watched as the mare's limbs took shape again in front of his eyes.

By day, as he had when he was taming his bay, he would work and run errands and clean the stables to repay old Pancia. Then every evening, when his arms and legs cried out for him to go home and rest, he would go to the stable, take out his purchase and work on her for an hour or two. By the time he got home, he barely had the strength to heat up a piece of meat or a plate of soup, and usually just collapsed on the kitchen table. More than once, his father had to lift him and throw him on the bed fully dressed. It was almost as if Daniel and Natan were no longer his sons, their father thought one evening, coming back to the living room to smoke his pipe by the fire after throwing Daniel on the bed. It was as if those two horses he had bought to keep them out of trouble had carried them off to a place he couldn't get into any longer.

One evening, old Pancia heard his name being called while his wife was finishing making dinner. Walking outside, the old man saw Daniel galloping his mare in the enclosure in the dim light.

The old man walked to the fence and leant on it. Daniel slowed down and came to a halt in front of him with a big smile on his face.

"What do you think?" Daniel risked asking.

Pancia smiled for a moment. "She's a fine animal," he said after a few seconds.

She was indeed a fine animal, finer than either he or the boy had imagined. Even the mare seemed to smile.

"What's her name?" old Pancia asked.

"First Deal," Daniel said, pleased with himself.

"First Deal?"

"Yes, First Deal," Daniel repeated.

The old man thought about it for a few seconds. "Rubbish name," he said, smiling again and turning to go back to his wife. As he was about to go inside, he turned to look at Daniel again.

"You never told me the name of your bay," he said.

Daniel had dismounted and was already taking the saddle off First Deal. "His name's Bay," Daniel said.

"Ah." Old Pancia shook his head and went back in to his wife.

NATAN WAS GOING TO THE CITY all the time now. He had found out the way to get through the hills at the far end of the valley and kept going back.

The first time Natan had come back from the city, he had immediately run to wake his brother.

"What is it?" Daniel had muttered.

"Wake up."

Daniel had turned over in bed and looked at his brother, who was standing there, very still. "What do you want?"

"Wake up."

"I'm already awake. What's the matter?"

"I've been to town."

"I know."

"You know?"

"Shit, Natan, you told me you were planning to go."

"But I didn't tell you I was definitely going."

"It's late, let me sleep."

"You don't know what it's like."

Daniel reopened his eyes and looked again at his brother standing there all excited and dirty. Suddenly he understood that his brother wasn't going away.

"Wait," he said finally.

Outside, in the meadow next to the farmyard, the two boys lay down and Natan started telling his brother all the things he had seen in the city, all the smells, the people hurrying along the streets, the inns every few metres, everyone shouting and screaming, the thousand sounds and colours and lights that came at you constantly from all sides, the girls of every shape and size, dressed in every

85

possible colour, the shops selling flowers, cakes, tools and everything you could ask for.

Natan kept his brother there until dawn, and in the end, when he couldn't take it any more, he said that everything he had just told him wasn't enough to describe a thousandth part of what you could find in a city. A whole lifetime wouldn't be enough, he said, to tell about all the things and people and stories you could find there.

When Natan had finished speaking, they lay there in silence for a few minutes. The blue light of dawn was already starting to appear behind the hills. Then Daniel got to his feet.

"I have to go to work," he said.

"You should come once," Natan said.

Daniel had nodded and helped his brother to get up. "See you later," he said.

Now Natan was spending more time in the city than anywhere else. He would disappear for weeks on end, then suddenly come back for two or three days, then disappear again.

Often he would come home with a few scratches on his face, or a black eye. Daniel knew he had been fighting again, but he didn't care. His brother had always been like that.

When Natan disappeared, though, it wasn't always to go to the city. Some people were ready to swear they had seen him sleeping with his horse in a clearing in the hills. Natan had always liked being on his own, he said that you could always rely on yourself, that however sick or twisted you were it always added up somehow. Daniel didn't know; he'd never thought about it.

Daniel never knew how Natan paid for his food. The only thing he knew for certain was that he never asked anyone for anything.

Once, their father had come to Daniel and asked him about his brother. Daniel had looked at him without knowing what to say.

"What do you want to know?" he asked.

For the first time in his life, Daniel had the impression that his father was floundering.

"I don't know. How does he live?"

Daniel wondered if the person in front of him was really his father. "He lives his own life," he said.

His father had nodded for a few seconds, then went away without a word.

A few evenings later, perhaps out of respect for this old man who resembled his father, Daniel had asked Natan how he was doing. Natan had looked at Daniel the same way Daniel must have looked at his father a few evenings earlier.

"I get by," Natan said. And that had been the end of the conversation.

DANIEL HAD IN FACT sometimes felt like following his brother to the city to see what it was like. A couple of times he had even been on the point of telling him, or stopping him when he saw him ride away on his chestnut. But every time he was about to open his mouth and get the words out, it was as if there was some kind of barrier stopping them, and he stood there watching the figure of his brother riding off along the road.

One evening when Natan was at home, Daniel went and found him in the stable, where he was giving his chestnut a last brush-down.

"Listen," Daniel said. "I need you to do me a favour."

Natan stopped brushing for a moment and gave him a puzzled look. "What kind of favour?"

"You have to come with me and do something."

"What?"

"You'll see."

Natan thought it over for a moment. "I'm tired," he said.

"So am I," Daniel said.

"All right," Natan said. "What do I have to do?"

"Saddle your horse, we're going to old Pancia's."

"My horse is tired, too."

"It won't kill him."

By the time they got to old Pancia's, it was after midnight and the almost full moon had spread a bluish-grey veil over the landscape.

"Wait here," Daniel said. "And don't make any noise."

He left the reins of his bay in his brother's hands and vanished behind old Pancia's house.

When he reappeared, he was leading another horse at the end of a rope.

"Who's he?" Natan asked when he came level.

"She. It's a mare."

"Who's she?" Natan said.

Daniel took the bay's reins off his hands and, still holding the rope that held First Deal, got back in the saddle. "She's mine."

"Yours?"

"Yes, mine."

"Since when?"

"A while."

Daniel gave a little kick with his legs and set off at a walking pace, with the mare behind him. They rode in silence in the moonlight for several minutes. It had been a while since they had last spent time together, and they both rather missed the times when they used to go out to the lake at night and go fishing. They could spend hours on end without talking, and it had seemed to them then that life could always be like that. But now it had changed a lot, in a way that neither of them had fully expected.

"Did you buy her?" Natan asked after a while.

Daniel nodded.

"Where did you get the money?"

"I worked and saved it."

For a moment, perhaps for the first time in his life, Natan felt something close to envy. "Did you have enough?"

"Old Pancia lent me a bit. But I didn't pay much, because she was sick. The owner thought she was dying and was going to send her to the abattoir."

"What happened?"

"We cured her."

Natan looked at his brother for a moment, then looked back at the road. "So you got a good deal," he said.

They fell silent again, and for a moment Natan felt like asking where they were going, but then he told himself it didn't make much difference.

They came to a clearing, which Natan did not recognise in the dim light. They descended a fairly steep path lined with bushes, at the bottom of which they caught a glimpse of a big stone house. When they reached the open space in front of the house, Daniel dismounted and looked around, then held out the reins and rope to his brother. Natan gave him a puzzled look, his hands resting on his chestnut's neck.

"Here," Daniel said under his breath. "Take the horses and go down there on the left. You'll see an enclosure. Wait for me there."

Natan took the reins and the rope. "And you?" he asked.

"I'll be there soon. Now go."

Natan watched as his brother walked towards the house, looking around him like a thief as he went. After a few steps Daniel stopped and turned back to look at his brother.

"Don't make a noise," he said, as if talking to a little boy, then continued walking towards the house.

Natan sat there for a few seconds, wondering what the hell his brother was up to. He looked down in the direction Daniel had pointed: a path descended on the left, with meadows on either side, and in the moonlight the grass and the horses' breath seemed like part of a painting.

At last, he made up his mind to move. He gave a tug on the ropes attached to Daniel's horses and turned his own chestnut towards the path.

This was the German's property. It was years since Natan had last been here, and in the meantime that weird foreigner who lived in the house had cleaned things up, planting grass and cutting down trees and bushes. Natan had the feeling of being in another country, as if someone had cut a piece off another part of the world and stuck it here without too much thought.

At the bottom of the path, on the right, Natan saw the enclosure Daniel had mentioned. He rode towards it, pulling his brother's horses behind him, looked around to make sure nobody was there, and dismounted. Calmly, he tied the three animals to the enclosure, took a packet of tobacco from his pocket, sat down on the fence and started rolling a cigarette. The next day he would go back to the city, he thought. He had already spent two or three days in these hills and he was starting to feel too clean. With the smoke from his mouth playing with the breeze and the moonlight, he wondered if one of these days he would go further than the city and see what there was beyond the mountains. He wondered if it was true what some people said: that if you kept going without ever stopping you'd end up back where you started. The first person to tell him that had been an old man with a beard, sitting in an inn. Natan had thought that was stupid: it seemed to him that if you kept going and didn't stop, you didn't know where you'd end up.

"The world is round," the old man had said, and that had somehow put an end to the conversation.

Natan heard a distant shuffling behind him. He turned and saw a horse descending from the house with a person attached. It was Daniel, who was trying with some difficulty to drag a huge horse as black as pitch. It took him several minutes to reach the enclosure. The big black horse kept shying and stopping and rushing forwards and breathing through his nose like a train. Digging in his heels, pulling on the rope and slapping the horse's neck, Daniel tried as best he could to restrain and orientate him.

When he came level with Natan, he told him, panting, to open the enclosure. Natan jumped down from the fence, ran to the opening, lifted the stakes and moved them aside, while Daniel tried to keep the black horse still.

"Go," Natan said when he had finished opening the enclosure.

Daniel glanced at it a couple of times as if measuring the opening, then in a single movement turned on his heels, ran a few steps, dragging the horse behind him, and threw him inside, untying the rope as he did so.

"Close it," he said immediately.

Natan rushed to close the enclosure as quickly as he could.

When he had finished, he turned and went to stand beside his brother. The black horse was bucking and kicking inside the enclosure, but gradually calming down. Daniel was leaning on the fence with his head down. His chest rose and fell rapidly as it used to do when they were children and they stopped after a long run.

"What now?" Natan asked, watching the splendid black horse as he gradually calmed down.

Daniel looked up at his brother. The moon and the stars seemed to be reflected in the sweat running down his face. "Do you think they heard us?" he asked, breathing just a little more slowly.

"Let's hope not," Natan said.

"Yes, let's hope not," Daniel replied, raising his eyes towards the black horse. "Beautiful, isn't he?"

Natan nodded. "Very," he said. "Are we stealing him?"

Daniel shot him a glance and smiled. "No, we're not stealing him."

"Pity," Natan said. "He's a beautiful animal."

Daniel walked around his brother and carried on to

where their horses were. He untied First Deal from the fence and led her back to the entrance of the enclosure. Natan laughed and went to open it.

"If the German finds out, he'll smash your head in," Natan said as his brother let the mare into the enclosure.

"Just imagine if we'd stolen him," Daniel said, happily. Natan gave another little laugh.

Natan and Daniel stood for a while leaning on the fence, looking into the enclosure, where the two horses slowly approached each other, blowing steam from their nostrils.

Natan put his hand in his pocket, took out the tobacco and started rolling another cigarette.

"Where did you get it?"

Natan looked up for a moment, as if not sure what Daniel was referring to. "In the city," he said.

For a few seconds, Daniel watched his brother fiddling with the tobacco and the little piece of paper as if he'd been doing it all his life. "Will you make me one, too?" he asked.

Natan looked up and lifted an eyebrow, as if to make sure that Daniel was really talking about a cigarette. "Sure," he said.

For a couple of minutes they watched the two horses slowly approach each other in the enclosure. From time to time their cigarettes would go out and have to be relit.

"It may be best to move the others away from the fence," Daniel said.

They took the bay and the chestnut and tied them to a tree some twenty or thirty metres further on. They loosened the saddle girths, gave the horses' necks a couple of slaps and went and lay down on the grass, each with one hand behind his head and the cigarette smoke drifting up towards the stars.

Daniel had never liked smoking, or at any rate had never had any great interest in it. But tonight was different. Tonight it was as if the city Natan had talked so much about was in the smoke that passed through his mouth and into his lungs.

It was as if all his brother's stories about the mixture of people and smells and sounds and colours had condensed into that thick tasty air that pounded his lungs and made his head feel light. This must be what being in the city was like: feeling dirty but happy. Over the years, whenever Daniel wanted to think about his brother, he would simply light a cigarette.

"It's good," Daniel said at last, lifting the cigarette slightly towards his brother.

"Yes, it's not bad," Natan said.

Daniel turned for a moment to look towards the enclosure, then stretched out again with one hand behind his head. "Have you ever done it?" he asked.

"What?"

"That."

Natan turned his head towards his brother, and saw that he was pointing behind them. He leant on his elbow and looked back. In the enclosure, First Deal seemed crushed by the huge black stallion, who was making great thrusts with his hind quarters. Natan gave a half-laugh and lay down again. "Sure," he said.

"Really?"

"Of course. There are loads of girls in the city. Loads of whores, too."

Daniel took a last drag on his cigarette, threw it far away and put his other hand behind his head.

"Why, haven't you?"

"No."

"Really?"

"Really."

Natan thought about it for a few seconds. "You should," he said.

"Right. And who with? There are no whores here."

"The pharmacist's daughter."

"The pharmacist's daughter? What the hell are you talking about? You think she's a whore?"

"Of course not. But I've seen the way she looks at you, like the other day when you went to get that stuff for old Pancia."

Daniel thought about it for a moment. "What do you mean, the way she looks at me?"

"You know, the way she looks at you."

"Really?"

"Yes, really."

"Are you sure?"

"Absolutely."

Daniel thought about it for another moment. "She's pretty, the pharmacist's daughter."

Natan glanced at his brother and for a moment thought he saw him smile. He nodded. "Very pretty."

They fell silent again for a few minutes, each thinking his own thoughts.

"And how is it?" Daniel asked.

Natan turned his head slightly, trying to understand what Daniel was referring to. "Warm," he said.

For another half-hour they lay on the grass in silence. Then Daniel raised himself on his elbow and looked to see what was happening in the enclosure. "Let's go," he said.

Natan turned and glanced back, too, then sat up, cracked his spine, and finally got to his feet. If it had been up to him, he would have stayed there till morning. They walked back to the enclosure.

"Take a rope and tie the mare," Daniel said. "I'll try and get the stallion."

First Deal let herself be taken almost at once. The stallion, though, tried to get away a few times, but in the end, with a bit of skill, Daniel managed to grab hold of him.

They repeated the previous operation in reverse: Natan opened the gate of the enclosure and Daniel led the stallion back up. In the meantime, Natan got the other horses and took them back towards the house, where he waited for his brother to return.

As he waited, Natan thought of rolling himself another cigarette. He had barely had time to put the tobacco in the paper when he heard a man shouting from somewhere behind the house. He turned abruptly and saw his brother emerge from behind the wall, running as fast as he could.

"Stop, you piece of shit!" he heard again from behind the house.

"Go, go, go!" Daniel yelled in an undertone as he came level. He mounted his bay as he did so, took the reins and rope from his brother's hands and set off at great speed. "Go!" he said again.

They heard more shouting. "STOP!"

A shot rang out. Natan could have sworn he felt bullets whistling past his ear. "Fuck this," he said, instinctively ducking his head and increasing speed.

Daniel laughed.

"Fuck off," Natan said.

They continued at a fast gallop until they came close to old Pancia's house. The hooves beat on the road like the drums in a band.

When they got home, after taking First Deal back to old Pancia's, they dismounted and started taking off the saddles.

"Do you think they recognised us?"

Daniel glanced at his brother. "Let's hope not."

They placed the saddles and bridles side by side on the fence and took the horses back to the stable. They put new water in the pails and hay in the manger. They gave the horses a few good slaps on their necks and walked back to the house.

"Thanks," Daniel said just before they went in.

"Don't mention it."

FORTUNATELY, First Deal had managed to get pregnant, and eleven months later gave birth to a splendid black colt. Daniel called him First Born.

Natan was hardly ever around any more. He'd grown a short beard like a sailor and spent all his time in the city, doing things no one knew about. From time to time, he would come back for a few days, spend all his time riding in the hills and then go away again saying he was going on a trip.

In the meantime, Daniel and the pharmacist's daughter had done what there was to do. Daniel spent all his free time with her. He would ride up to her house on his bay, let her climb up behind him, and take her somewhere in the countryside. They talked about houses and children and a life together, and whenever Daniel felt sick he would go to her house to be seen to. This was the way life could be, Daniel thought.

One day they were in the inn, sitting at a wooden table in the corner, having soup.

Daniel and the girl heard a commotion from the other side of the room. There at the counter was the man who had sold Daniel First Deal. He was talking excitedly and was being held back by a couple of friends. After a few seconds he broke free, walked heavily across the room and up to Daniel's table. He had the watery eyes and lopsided stride of someone who has been drinking too much.

"You stole my horse, you bastard," he said when he was level with Daniel.

Daniel glanced at him. "I didn't steal anything," he said.

One of the man's friends came over and took his arm. "Let's go," he said. "We can sort this out another time."

"No!" the first man said, pulling his arm away. "This bastard stole a mare from me and then sneaked over and got her pregnant with the German's stallion."

"I didn't steal anything. I paid for that mare."

"A pittance!"

"She was sick. You were going to send her to the abattoir."

"You knew you could cure her," the man muttered.

"No, I hoped I could," Daniel said, glancing again at the man, then took another sip of his soup. "Go home," he said. "You're drunk."

The man stood there for a couple of seconds, as stiff as a log, and stared at Daniel with his drink-sodden eyes. Then he turned and saw a big glass tankard someone had left on a table beside him. It all happened in a moment, and Daniel did not even have time to raise his hand, but he would remember every instant: the man's twisted fingers tightening round the tankard, the fingertips and the palm of the hand turning white with the pressure, the tankard coming off the table and leaving a round puddle on the surface, the muscles of the man's arm tightening, his left foot shifting forwards, his face screwing up with the effort and the anger, those dozens of lines on it like a crumpled leaf, the remains of the froth in the tankard as it came closer, the cold glass against his left eye, the explosion of glass in little drops and that suspended moment when it seemed to him that he was seeing an enchanted world. Then the darkness and his own hands on his face and that sensation like a hundred burning coals. The last thing Daniel remembered was the pharmacist's daughter screaming.

The girl rushed to Daniel, who was lying on the ground unconscious, his face covered in blood. The man's friends dragged him outside. He was still waving his arms about and threatening to finish what he had started, but he didn't sound very convinced any more.

The innkeeper ran out from behind the counter with a cloth in his hand, and went and pressed it to Daniel's face.

"Let's take him to my house," the pharmacist's daughter said.

The innkeeper nodded, crouched down and took Daniel in his arms.

The pharmacist did not know what to think when he saw his daughter come in with the innkeeper carrying a wounded boy in his arms. He preferred not to think about what his daughter had to do with all that blood.

"Come in, put him in there," the pharmacist said to the innkeeper, pointing to a door on the other side of the kitchen.

The innkeeper went through the door and laid Daniel on the big bed that was there.

"Fetch the doctor," the pharmacist said at last, going to Daniel to get a better look at him. The innkeeper nodded without a word and ran out. The pharmacist carefully turned Daniel's head and lifted the bloodstained cloth from his face. A long black cut, gaping like a toothless grin, descended from his left eyebrow to just above his jaw.

"Go into the shop," the pharmacist said to his daughter without taking his eyes off Daniel. "Get some disinfectant, some gauze, a needle and some suturing thread, a pair of sterile scissors and some plaster. Then put some water on to boil."

"Is he going to be all right?" his daughter asked.

"Hurry up," he said.

When his daughter came back, he took some gauze and disinfectant and tried to clean the wound.

A few minutes later the doctor arrived. "What happened?" he asked, approaching the bed with his bag in his hand.

"He's got a nasty wound," the pharmacist said.

The doctor put the bag down next to the bed and leant over Daniel. He put his hands on his face and squeezed the wound in a few places. The blood came out again like water from a weir.

"Needle and thread?" the doctor asked.

"Here they are," the pharmacist said.

The doctor turned and glanced at the pharmacist's needle and thread. "Good," he said.

By the time the doctor had finished an hour later, a crooked line of stitches ran down Daniel's face. The doctor went and washed his hands, then came back into the room, rolled down his sleeves and started putting his coat back on.

"Give him an injection for the pain and let him rest," he said, picking up his bag.

The pharmacist nodded and walked the doctor to the door. When he came back, his daughter was still there, looking at Daniel. Her eyes were still swollen.

"Go to bed," her father said curtly.

It took Daniel a few seconds to realise what that white-hot dagger he could feel stuck to his face was, and longer still to try and work out where he was. Slivers of colour floated in front of him as soon as he closed his eyes, and it seemed to him as if his heart was throbbing beneath the skin of his face, trying to rip through the flesh and get out. He touched his face with his hand and felt the gauze over the whole of the left side. In a flash, he remembered the tankard and the rain of glass exploding like a firework. But that was all.

He tried to recall some other memory, some other image or sound that might give him an idea of where he was. He turned his head towards the window. A pale blue and yellow light was starting to be visible beyond the hills, which stood out against the sky like a piece of cardboard. It looked like being a nice sunny day and he felt like laughing, but if he as much as smiled it was like a red-hot dagger turning in his flesh.

He pulled himself up into a sitting position and sat there for a couple of minutes with his elbows on his knees. All he wanted was for his heart to leave his face alone and go back to his chest. He got to his feet, picked up his trousers from a chair in the corner of the room, put them on, pulled on his boots, tried to crack his spine, and went and opened the door.

He saw a dark, bare corridor with a couple of prints on the wall. On the left of the corridor, a series of doors, closed except for one, through which he glimpsed the arm of an armchair. On the right, the corridor led to what looked like a kitchen and on the other side of the kitchen what looked like a door leading outside.

Daniel touched the gauze lightly with his fingertips, waited a few seconds, and finally headed for the kitchen. His legs felt heavy, as if two ten-kilo sacks were tied to them, and apart from the pain his face now felt unpleasantly itchy. If he closed his eyes, those damn slivers of colour floated in front of him again.

Slowly, he managed to get through the kitchen and reach the door. He liked this kitchen, he thought, it had a homely feel.

"You should rest," a voice said behind him.

The pharmacist was standing in the door from the corridor, still as a statue, his hands in his pockets, staring at him without expression.

It took Daniel a few seconds to put everything together, and he never took his eyes off the man's. "I can't," he said at last. "But thanks all the same."

Then he turned and opened the door to go out.

"We need to talk," the pharmacist said.

Daniel turned back to look at him. "I know," he said. "I'll be back."

The pharmacist nodded, and after a couple of seconds Daniel managed to get through the door and close it behind him.

Fortunately, his bay was there, outside the house. He gathered what strength he seemed to have left, put the saddle on the horse, tightened the girth as much as he could, and got on.

He let the horse take him to old Pancia's house. He could not keep his left eye open, and if it had not been for those damn slivers of colour he would have kept the other one closed, too. As the bay carried him calmly towards old Pancia's, the morning light was starting to illumine and cool the countryside. Daniel remembered his brother's cigarettes: now would have been the perfect moment to smoke one, he thought. It was as if something was missing from the dawn and the steam from the bay's nostrils and the bandage on his face and the eye that didn't want to stay open, and a cigarette would certainly have completed the picture. Life was always like that, Daniel thought: something was always missing, whereas the nice thing about stories was that everything that should be there was there.

When Daniel reached old Pancia's, the house was still shrouded in silence. The only sound was the song of two hoopoes somewhere nearby. It was day now, and after the dawn frost the air had already started to warm up. No sooner had the bay's hooves started to beat on the gravel leading to the house than old Pancia came out through the door with a steaming cup in his hand and his shirt hanging down over his belly as usual like a skirt.

"You're early this morning," old Pancia said, taking a sip from the steaming cup. Then he saw Daniel's gauze and the closed eye and the purplish-blue tinge that coloured half his face.

"Good heavens, son, what have you done?"

Old Pancia walked forwards quickly, took hold of the bay's bridle and watched as Daniel dismounted with difficulty.

"Never mind," Daniel said.

The boy left the bay where he was, in the open space in front of the house, and walked towards the stables. "Didn't you hear anything last night?" he asked old Pancia.

"No. What happened?"

"Never mind."

Daniel reached the stable and opened the little gate. In the second box, First Deal was lying on the straw in a pool of blood, her neck slashed. She didn't look like herself any more, she was like some grotesque life-size rag doll. And that big cut on her neck, at least two hands long, looked as if it had been sliced in rubber. Only the blood gave the impression that everything was real.

"Shit," Daniel said. He tilted his head to one side and held it with one hand, lightly squeezing his closed eyelids.

He stood like that, without moving, as if something had become jammed.

"What are you going to do?" old Pancia asked.

"I don't know," Daniel replied, without moving or opening his eyes.

After a few more minutes, old Pancia had the impression that Daniel had nodded. Then he lifted his head, walked out of the stable, told the old man that he would be back later, got calmly back on his horse and rode off.

DANIEL RODE ALL THE WAY HOME, went in, took a rifle from the rack, found two cartridges in the drawer of the cabinet and loaded them in the gun. When his father saw him, he asked him what he was planning to do. Daniel turned and looked at him with his one good eye.

"Don't worry, Dad."

His father had often thought that something like this would happen one day. He had felt it since the day his wife had died and he had felt alone and had seen the two boys going off alone through the countryside. He had never thought, though, that it would happen to Daniel. He would have expected to see Natan come back one day dying or covered in blood, with the police after him. But he would never have thought that it would happen to this other son who had bought a horse with his own money and who got up every day at dawn to work. He wondered if he ought to do something, or stop Daniel from doing something, but he had a kind of feeling that his son had understood what he was thinking. Then it struck him that it had been a while now since, without saying anything, each of them had chosen to live his own life, and that it was pointless to do anything.

"Don't do anything stupid," he said, letting him pass.

"Don't worry," Daniel replied, dragging himself outside. He was hungry, but he would eat later, he thought.

When Daniel got to the farm where he had bought First Deal, there didn't seem to be anyone around, and the sun was high in the sky by that time, which made things more difficult.

Daniel settled down with his bay, right in the middle of the open space in front of the big reddish house, with his rifle resting across the animal's neck.

After a few minutes, the man who had sold him First Deal emerged. He also had a rifle in his hand, and was followed by three other men with bowed legs and weathered skin. Two of them were the men who had been present almost two years earlier when the mare was sold.

They all stood there motionless for a couple of minutes, not sure how to act.

"What are we going to do?" Daniel said, without moving.

The man who had sold him First Deal waited a few seconds and tried to swallow. He didn't like this situation at all.

Another man came out through the front door. He was wearing a white shirt and a nice greenish jacket. His grey hair was combed back as if it was sculpted, and a small beard outlined his jaw as precisely as a ruler. "Tonino," he said.

The man who had sold First Deal to Daniel turned abruptly. He looked worried.

"What's going on?" the man in the shirt and jacket asked.

The man called Tonino turned back and looked fixedly at Daniel. "This kid stole a horse from us, sir."

The man in the jacket took his eyes off Tonino and looked at Daniel. He took a couple of steps forwards. "Is this true?" he asked.

"No, sir, it isn't true." Daniel said. "I bought and paid for the horse, sir, fair and square. These men are my witnesses." He pointed to the men behind Tonino.

The man in the jacket turned to the two men. "Is this true?" he asked.

"She was sick," Tonino snarled without lowering his rifle, "and he bought her at the same price the abattoir would have paid. But he knew how to cure her and didn't say anything. Then he sneaked over to the German's place and had her mounted by the German's stallion and she had a colt. He tricked all of us."

"Sir," Daniel said, "I suspected the mare could be cured, but I wasn't sure. If she hadn't recovered, I would have sold her to the abattoir myself. It was the only way I could buy a horse, sir. Luckily she did recover, but I bought her and paid for her."

The man in the jacket turned to Tonino's two companions. "Is this true?" he asked.

One of the two looked at him as timidly as a little boy. "He never said she could be cured," he said.

The man in the jacket seemed to be getting annoyed. He turned to Daniel again and was silent for a few seconds, as if weighing up what to do.

"As far as the German's stallion is concerned, sir, it's true I went over there at night and had the mare mounted. But as soon as possible I would have found a way to repay the German. You can ask anyone, sir, I'm an honest person."

The man looked at the bandaged boy and Tonino and their rifles. There was something in all this that still escaped him. "Well, then?" he asked, as if addressing all of them. "What's the problem?"

Daniel looked him in the eyes for a couple of seconds. "The problem, sir, is that I've paid with half my face and the mare."

"The mare?"

"Yes, sir. She died with her throat cut in old Pancia's stable. I'm an honest person, sir, but I won't work my arse off for nothing."

The white haired man looked at him gravely. "What about your face?"

"Ask him," Daniel said, indicating Tonino with his chin.

The man turned to Tonino. "Well?" he said.

"He tricked us," Tonino said curtly.

The man looked Daniel in the eyes again for a few seconds, and for a moment it seemed to him that there was something romantic in the boy's tired look, the closed eye, the bandage and the rifle resting on the horse's neck.

"Tonino," the man said. "Go and get our brood mare and bring her here."

Tonino turned to the man and looked at him in astonishment.

"Move," the man said.

Tonino looked at the man for another couple of seconds, then shook his head, spat on the ground, and walked round to the other side of the house.

A few minutes later, he came back leading a big grey horse at the end of a rope.

"Give her to him," the man said, when Tonino had come closer.

Tonino stopped dead, as if to say something.

"Give her to him," the man said.

Tonino walked right up to Daniel and held out the rope without even looking at him.

"She's a good brood mare," the man said. "I'm going to have a word with the German. He'll let you have the mare mounted as often as you like, you'll see."

"Thank you, sir."

The man nodded gravely, then looked at Tonino again. "Give me the rifle," he said.

Tonino took three steps forwards and held out the rifle to the man.

"Now, Tonino, you have fifteen minutes to pack your things and get out."

Tonino looked at the man in amazement. "But, sir—"

"Don't fucking 'sir' me. I paid you to look after my horses. You sold a good mare at a price you'd have got from an abattoir without knowing she could be cured. And you just lost me a good brood mare to settle your debt. Not to mention what you did to this boy and his horse. I'll be back in fifteen minutes. If I see you here or anywhere in the vicinity I swear I'll shoot you in the legs."

Daniel decided he had no great desire to stick around and see what was going to happen, it wasn't his business, so he said goodbye, turned the horses and set off the way he had come.

"Goodbye," the man said gravely, without taking his eyes off Tonino.

B Y THE TIME Natan returned to the area, the purple marks on Daniel's face had faded, leaving only a few faint blue and yellow patches. His eye, fortunately, had opened and didn't cause him any trouble, and he only kept the bandage on his face to cover the nasty-looking stitches. The doctor had told him they could come out, too, in a few days.

It was late afternoon and Daniel was giving his bay a last brush-down.

Natan approached, tied his chestnut to the enclosure and started undoing the saddle. "Hi," he said.

"Hi," he heard Daniel say, then saw his bandaged, disfigured face emerge from behind the horse.

Natan felt as if a hand was squeezing his stomach. "What the fuck happened?"

Daniel glanced at him and continued brushing his bay. "Nothing, Natan, don't worry."

"Tell me."

"It was nothing. Forget it."

Natan felt a tingling sensation starting in his stomach and moving out along his arms. "Tell me what happened."

"Forget it, Natan, it's not your business."

Natan thought about it for a few seconds, then spat on the ground. "Shit," he said. Then he went and sat down on the fence and started rolling a cigarette. "Does it hurt?" he asked after a while.

Daniel smiled for a moment. "Not any more," he said.

"Can I see?"

Daniel stopped brushing the horse down and walked to the fence, calmly taking the bandage from his face as he did so, then stopped in front of Natan with his head slightly tilted to one side and his eye closed.

"Shit," Natan said.

There was a reddish line all the way down his face, surrounded by little pieces of black thread.

"Can I?" Natan said, raising his hand.

Daniel nodded without a word. Gently, Natan touched the wound with one finger. It was like being a giant and moving your finger over a dirt road.

The wound seemed to have a voice, and a story to tell.

"Shit," Natan said, taking his finger away and standing there for another few seconds admiring the wound.

"Nice, isn't it?" Daniel said.

Natan nodded without a word.

The following day Daniel got up at dawn as usual and went to work at old Pancia's. Around mid-morning, Natan rode up on his chestnut. Daniel was taking the horses out to clean the stable.

"Hey," Natan said.

"Hey," Daniel replied.

"I'm going on a little trip."

Daniel stopped and gave him a puzzled look. He had never come to say goodbye before.

"Oh," Daniel said, looking his brother in the eyes. "All right."

"Who's she?" Natan asked, indicating the new grey mare with his chin.

Daniel turned to the mare. "They gave her to me to replace First Deal."

"What happened to First Deal?"

"First Deal died."

"Oh," Natan said. "And what's this one called?"

"This one's called Substitute," Daniel said, giving the mare's neck a couple of slaps.

Natan gave a half-laugh. "OK," he said. "I'm off."

Daniel nodded. "See you soon."

Natan nodded, too. "Yes, see you soon," he said, then after a couple of seconds turned his chestnut and slowly rode away.

Daniel watched him until he vanished from sight at the end of the road. He had the feeling the trip would be longer than usual this time.

THE MONKEY

W HEN THE PHONE RANG, Nico was busy playing Subbuteo. He was expecting an important call from his
agent and while waiting had decided that instead of wasting the afternoon he would get out that old green box from
the back of the wardrobe. It had been a birthday present
from his sister a couple of years earlier. He had never learnt
how to play Subbuteo, and ever since he was a child he had
envied those friends of his who spent their afternoons bent
over a plywood surface and the next day at school talked
about their matches as if they'd been playing in the World
Cup finals. That green box, those plywood shelves and those
little men on their tumblers had always aroused in him the
same embarrassing envy as table football. You're not really
a man if you can't play Subbuteo and table football, he had
always thought, and it was a complex that had somehow
stayed with him all his life.

When his sister had given him the Subbuteo set, Nico's
first thought had been that there was some kind of sinister
ulterior motive behind the gift—but then he'd thought,
Who cares? and had again promised himself to learn as
soon as he could. But the box had ended up at the back of
the wardrobe. When you get down to it, we are what we
are. That afternoon, though, had seemed like a good time
to do something about his old resolutions.

Nico walked nonchalantly to the low table on which the
phone stood, without taking his eyes off the Subbuteo mat
and those tiny coloured players.

"Hello, Angela?"

"Hi, Nico. It's Maria."

"You're not Angela?"

117

"No, I'm Maria."

"Shit, I was hoping you were Angela."

"Sorry about that. I can try and play her part if you like, even though I don't know her. Who is she?"

"My agent. I'm expecting some important news."

"I'm sorry I'm not her."

"Yes, so am I." He thought for a moment. "Sorry, but Maria who?"

At the other end of the line, Nico heard the hint of an unconvincing laugh. "Piero's sister."

"Piero's sister?"

"Yes, you remember Piero, your friend Piero?"

"Yes, of course, it's just that ... Never mind. How are you?"

The first time Nico had seen Maria she had been half-lying on a small wicker sofa in her garden, reading a thick paperback novel. She was wearing a light yellow dress that moved slightly in the breeze, and a wide-brimmed straw hat shaded her face from the sun. She looked like something out of a story by F Scott Fitzgerald. Nico had immediately fallen in love with her, and for years Maria had been his erotic fantasy, the inaccessible, almost mystical creature everyone encounters some time during their adolescence.

"Not bad," Maria said. "And you?"

"Oh, not bad. You know how it is ... "

"Of course," Maria said with a smile in her voice.

Nico thought it unlikely that that almost unreal creature with all those eccentric friends and that glittering life really knew how it was, but when you get down to it that's the kind of thing people say.

"How's work?" Maria asked. Some people had a particular way of saying the word "work", an imperceptible change of rhythm which made it sound ridiculous.

"Pretty good. I'm expecting a call from my agent, but, you know, everything's going along OK."

"It must be interesting work."

"I don't know about that," Nico said. "Better than working down a mine, though."

Maria gave a half-laugh, Nico gave a half-laugh, and then they both let that trite remark drift off into silence.

"Listen, Nico, I need to talk to you about my brother."

"Yes, of course. What is it, has he run away again? I haven't seen him. Haven't even heard from him for about a month-and-a-half. I know you two were supposed to be going on holiday together."

"Yes … No … The thing is … Listen, Piero has started acting like a monkey."

"Started doing what?"

"Acting like a monkey."

"Like a monkey? I'm sorry, how do you mean?"

"I mean some time this summer he started bending double and grunting like a monkey. It was funny at first, we thought it was a game, but then he wouldn't stop."

Nico said nothing for a long time. Odd coloured images of his friend passed in front of his eyes, followed by images of monkeys, but he couldn't seem to fit the two things together.

"Nico, are you still there?"

"Yes, it's just that … "

"Yes, I know," Maria said.

Nico was silent again for a few seconds. "It's just that I find it hard to imagine."

"Yes, I realise that."

The thing Maria probably didn't realise was that what Nico found really strange wasn't this business with Piero but the fact of being on the phone with her. It was as if the monkey story had immediately been relegated to some surreal, comical region which had little to do with reality.

"I was thinking perhaps you could come here and see him."

Nico sank into the armchair and almost laughed.

"Nico, are you there?"

"Yes," Nico said, trying to hold back his laughter. At that moment, the idea of going to see a friend of his who was acting like a monkey seemed ridiculous, nothing more. And his sister's grave tone even more so. "I'll come as soon as I can," he said. "I just need to sort out a few things here."

"Great, we'll be waiting."

Nico put down the phone and sat there looking at the receiver. After a few minutes, he took an old, chewed-up orange pencil from the little table next to the armchair, one of the ones he liked to draw with from time to time. He stuck the pencil between his teeth and looked around the room, lost in thought. Every object he rested his eyes on seemed to have some more or less direct connection with Piero.

It was as if after a while some people got inside you and somehow remained forever part of what you were and what you did, even if you hardly ever saw them. It was as if despite himself that boisterous friend he'd practically grown up with but now almost never saw was an integral part of what he was.

Nico looked at the telephone again, lifted the receiver and dialled a number.

"Hello?"

"Hi, Angela, it's Nico."

"Hi, Nico."

"Any news?"

"Nico, you called me half-an-hour ago."

"Yes, I know. Any news?"

"No, no news."

"Nothing from Star Films?"

"Were you expecting news from somewhere else?"

"No, I don't think so."

"No, there's nothing from Star Films. Are you planning to call me every half-hour until we hear something? It could take days, you know."

Nico imagined Angela sitting comfortably in her leather armchair in her splendid office overlooking the Tiber. He could just see her sitting there with the receiver wedged between her head and her shoulder, making bored little noises and sarcastic faces as she spoke, especially if her secretary was there. Angela wasn't exactly what you'd call friendly, but there was something about her and her sarcastic manner that Nico couldn't do without. She was one of those overweight women with their wombs full of cement who at some point in their lives have decided that a good business deal is better than sleeping with a man. One of those emancipated women who can't cook and don't read books, but who go around with big Hermès scarves round their necks and save face by reading the arts pages of the weekend financial paper. Basically, Nico wasn't supposed to go to bed with her, and all Angela had to do was get him as much money as she could, which was why the fact that she had a womb full of cement and put a good business deal before anything else wasn't such a bad thing when you got down to it.

"No, listen, I just wanted to tell you I have to go home for the weekend. Is that going to be a problem?"

"I don't know, are you asking me if the city will miss you?"

"Angela, do me a favour … I was thinking about Star Films."

"Apparently they've invented these things called mobile phones, you have heard of them, haven't you?"

"You know I don't have one."

"Maybe it's time you did."

"I doubt it, but I'll think about it."

"Great, welcome to the twenty-first century."

For a few seconds, Nico said nothing, just chewed his pencil. "You know, I'm going to see a friend of mine who's started acting like a monkey."

Nico wondered why he had said that, but then it occurred to him that he was curious to know her reaction.

"Oh," Angela said. "Have fun."

"Is that all?"

"What do you mean, 'Is that all?'"

"I told you I'm going to see a friend of mine who's started acting like a monkey."

"Yes, I heard you."

"Don't you think that's odd?"

"To tell the truth, I don't really give a shit."

"But he really has started acting like a monkey, grunting, that kind of thing."

"Well, that's fine, but—"

"What would you do?"

"What do you mean?"

"If a friend of yours started acting like a monkey."

"Nico, I have no idea. I'm your agent, not your analyst."

"Fuck it, Angela, you must have an opinion."

"Nico, don't raise your voice to me."

"I'm sorry."

"Forget it."

Silence.

"So?"

"So what?"

"This friend of mine. The one who's started acting like a monkey."

"Nico, I don't know. This is turning into a really weird conversation, and I hate weird conversations."

"So that's your get-out, is it?"

"What do you mean, my get-out?"

"A friend of yours starts acting like a monkey and the most intelligent thing you can think of to say is 'I hate weird conversations'."

"No, that's what I'm saying to you, because I don't have any friends who've started acting like monkeys."

"Yes, but—"

"Nico, roll yourself a joint, they say it helps. Now, look, I'm sorry, but I really have to go, I'm very busy, I have to keep this show on the road. Take care." And she put down the phone.

Nico stared at the receiver for a moment or two, then calmly put it back. He remembered that in films they always put down the receiver without saying goodbye, and that he'd always thought this the height of bad manners. And in fact, it really wasn't nice, especially when it was your agent who did it. Nico knew other people who had agents, and they all spoke about them almost as friends. Nico had wondered if it was normal for his agent to take the liberties she did, or treat everyone with that kind of maternal arrogance. In the end, Nico had thought about it and concluded that he preferred it this way, and that the last thing he wanted from his agent was a hypocritical show of friendship.

Nico put the pencil back in his mouth and thought again about the story of Piero and the monkey. He wondered what his reaction should be to a piece of news like that, if it was right to feel that strange euphoria which had been his first reaction. He wondered if he ought instead to be worried, or upset, or if he should feel as if a burden had been placed on his shoulders. He often wondered if he had the right reaction to dramatic or intense events that affected his life. At that moment, all he felt was curiosity, a cheerful, almost euphoric interest in an event which, one way or another, would add some colour to his otherwise monochrome life.

All of a sudden, he felt the impulse to go back to his home town and see how things really were. He wanted to know if it was still possible to be surprised. He lifted the receiver again and dialled a number.

"Hello?"

"Hi."

"Hi."

"How are you?"

"Fine. What's the matter?"

Nico decided to approach things in a roundabout way. "I was just calling to see how you were," he said.

"Well, pretty much the same as I was an hour ago. What is it, darling?"

"Nothing, I just wanted to hear your voice."

"Is that all?"

"Yes, pretty much."

"But there's something else."

"No, not really, it's just that I have to go home today."

"What?"

"I have to go—"

"Yes, I heard what you said. No way."

"Something's happened that's out of my control."

"Oh, yes? And what would that be?"

"A friend of mine has started acting like a monkey."

There was a moment's silence.

"That's the dumbest excuse I've ever heard. You know something? Your little fantasies don't make me laugh the way they used to."

Nico moved the receiver away from his ear for a moment

and looked up at the ceiling. "I swear to you, it's the truth," he said. "His sister just called me."

"And who is this friend?"

"His name's Piero."

"And how come whenever we want to go away for the weekend, you always come out with some story about a friend?"

"I have a lot of friends."

"Don't be a bastard, Nico."

Nico screwed up his eyes and tried to stay calm. "But I'm sure I've talked to you about this one."

"A friend of yours who behaves like a monkey? I don't think so. I have a feeling I'd have remembered something like that."

"He didn't use to behave like a monkey. He only started this summer."

"And before that, what did this friend do?"

"You mean, what work did he do?"

"Yes."

"Why?"

"Nico, don't mess me about."

"He's done a bit of everything."

"I've never heard of this friend of yours, and you can't even think up a plausible profession for him. I keep telling you, I can't stand lies."

"I've never lied to you."

"So you say."

It was frustrating. However hard Nico thought about it, he couldn't remember when and where this thing about lies had started. All he knew was that overnight his witty, understanding, tolerant girlfriend had turned suspicious and started questioning everything he told her. She had convinced herself that he was lying to her. At first, Nico had thought it was a phase, maybe she was a little stressed out and just needed to let off steam. But then it had continued, so Nico had tried telling some real lies. It had worked.

Today, though, he'd thought he'd be honest.

"It's that strange, brilliant friend of mine who's been a painter, among other things."

"Oh, the one whose father died. The one who's done all kinds of things?"

"Yes, that's right, that one. You see, you do remember."

"I've never been convinced about this friend of yours."

Nico lowered the receiver and held it against his thigh, glancing to one side in exasperation, as if someone was in the room with him. There were times when he found her suspicions, her incredulity, quite endearing, but this wasn't one of them. Right now, all he really wanted to do was have a little laugh with his girlfriend about Piero who had started acting like a monkey, then hang up and run and catch the first train to his home town.

"Listen, Giada, let's not fuck around," Nico said. "What's eating you? To be honest, I'm not in the mood for games right now. Why do you have to come out with this crap?"

"Because every time we're supposed to be doing something nice to pick up the pieces of our relationship, something comes up that you can't postpone."

"I didn't know we were trying to pick up the pieces of our relationship."

"Then what were we going down to Naples for, can you tell me that?"

"Maybe to have a weekend by the sea before it gets cold?"

"I don't think so."

"Oh. Obviously I missed something."

"I'm sorry, but hadn't you noticed I've been particularly affectionate to you in the last few days?"

"Actually, I had, and I wonder what happened to the woman who brought me coffee in bed this morning. Could you put her on? She must be there somewhere."

"Don't be a bastard, Nico."

"Giada, I don't follow you. I really don't see the connection between this fit of temper of yours, Naples, your affectionate behaviour and the fact that we're supposed to be mending our relationship."

"Nico, why do you think I've been so nice to you lately?"

"I don't suppose a simple answer like 'just to be nice' will do, will it?"

"No, not really."

Nico screwed up his eyes. He felt tired. He would have liked to just drop the receiver on the armchair and go out without even closing the door. "So tell me, because I can't figure it out," he said with a sigh.

"I've been especially nice to give a boost to our relationship."

Nico again tried to find a connection between the alleged crisis in their relationship, Giada's affectionate behaviour, and their weekend in Naples, and for a moment he felt as though he was part of a show he hadn't even known existed. He waited a few seconds, moving his fingers over his closed eyelids.

"I'm sorry, Giada," he said at last. "Isn't there anything you women can do without all this mental masturbation?"

"Go to hell, Nico."

For the second time in barely a handful of minutes, Nico heard the phone being slammed down on him. This time, though, he felt a hint of childish satisfaction.

Nico put the receiver back calmly, then wondered again what he should think about this story of Piero, whether he should feel annoyed because it had already caused problems for him with both his agent and his girlfriend, or whether he should thank him for having brightened up his day from one moment to the next. He also wondered why Giada had got so hot under the collar about this story of the monkey and their weekend in Naples. He wondered if it might be the result of some hormonal upheaval, some typical women's problem, like premature menopause.

He turned, picked up his address book from the little table, leafed through it and, with the receiver wedged between his head and his shoulder, dialled another number.

"Good afternoon, surgery."

"Could I speak to the doctor, please?"

"Who shall I say is calling?"

"Her ex."

"One moment, please."

For some reason, Nico felt pleased to have introduced himself as the doctor's ex. After a few moments, someone came on the line.

"Hello?"

"Hi, Chiara, it's Nico."

"Hi, Nico. Do you usually call people at work and introduce yourself as their ex?"

"No, it's the first time I've ever done that, but I like it. I think I'll do it more often."

"There's an idea. How are you?"

"Not bad. Listen, Chiara, is it possible for a thirty-year-old woman to have an attack of premature menopause?"

"Nico, to begin with, it's not possible to have an *attack* of menopause, plus I think it's rather unlikely at the age of thirty. Why?"

"Just wondering. And listen, that time we went to Paris together, did we go because we needed to mend our relationship?"

"No, we went because we wanted to visit Euro Disney."

"Was that all?"

128

"Yes, that was all."

That was all. Nico seemed to hear a Rossini aria playing around those words. There still existed women who could say them.

"Chiara," Nico said, "how come you and I split up?"

"You met someone else, Nico."

"Oh, so I did. I'm sorry."

"Don't worry. I met someone else, too."

"Oh, good. And how was it?"

"Fine. Actually, we got married. We have two children now."

For a moment, Nico envied this man he didn't know, and saw himself happily married with a family. Then part of him wondered if that was why he had gone and found someone else—though he couldn't remember who.

"Really?" Nico said. "That's wonderful. I don't suppose there's any chance of us getting back together, then?"

Chiara laughed. "No, I don't think so. But if you want to come over for dinner, I'd like that."

"I'll think about it."

Silence.

"Girlfriend problems?"

"Yes, but that's not the only thing. A friend of mine has started acting like a monkey."

"What?"

"A friend of mine has started acting like a monkey."

"How do you mean?"

"I mean he's started grunting and acting like a monkey. Sounds to me as if he's gone mad."

"Shit," Chiara said. Nico heard her apologising to someone and asking them to wait another moment. Then she said, "I'm so sorry, Nico."

"Yes, I know, it's really weird. But who knows, maybe it's better this way."

"Yes, maybe," Chiara said, sounding unconvinced.

Nico and Chiara were silent for a moment.

"Nico, I'm sorry, but I really have to go. I'm in the middle of a consultation."

"You mean, while we've been talking, you've been staring at a patient's pussy?"

"Yes."

"What a great job you have. Is it a nice one?"

"Bye, Nico."

"Bye, Chiara, take care."

As he put down the receiver, Nico heard Chiara laugh. It was always a nice feeling, making a woman laugh.

NICO SPENT MUCH OF THE TRAIN JOURNEY in the bar with a beer in front of him, staring out at the trees and hills and tunnels and roads parading past him. He was trying not to think of anything—not Angela, not the phone call he was expecting from Star Films, not how he would pay the bills and the rent if it didn't come, not Giada, not the weekend in Naples, not the coffee she'd brought him in bed that morning, not that final "Go to hell". Above all, he was trying not to think about Piero. He didn't want to spoil that tangible, if weird, story—assuming it was all true—with some pointless fake image from his own imagination.

When he reached his destination, he got in the first taxi he found and gave the driver the address of Piero's house.

"Is that your house?" the driver asked as they set off.

Nico took his eyes off the stream of people outside and looked at the driver in the rear-view mirror. "I'm sorry, what did you say?"

"The address. Is that your house?"

"No," Nico said. "A friend of mine's."

The driver nodded and glanced at Nico in the mirror. "A pity," he said. "It's a good address."

Nico gave a little laugh. "Yes, a pity," he said. When you really got down to it, seeing how things had turned out, he wasn't convinced it was such a pity, but there you were.

"He's started acting like a monkey," Nico said.

The driver looked at him again in the rear-view mirror. He had deep-set black eyes surrounded by dozens of lines. He must have laughed a lot in his life.

"What do you mean?" the driver asked.

131

"My friend. This summer he started acting like a monkey, and hasn't stopped. I'm going to visit him, to see if he's getting back to normal."

The driver looked at him again in the rear-view mirror. "They think of all sorts these days," he said after a few seconds.

Nico threw him a glance and wondered what he meant. He was almost on the verge of asking him, but then he told himself that some things are better left as they are, and anyway he didn't much feel like talking. He looked out of the window again. The taxi had already left the centre of town and was starting to drive up into the hills, and the faded light of late afternoon gave everything the intense, vaguely melancholy air of a grand finale.

When they reached the gate, the taxi driver asked Nico if he wanted to be taken all the way up to the house. No, there was no need, Nico said, and he paid, said thank you and got out. He stood there for a few moments watching the taxi turn and head back down along the tarred road lined by the stone walls of the gardens of villas.

Nico turned to face the huge gate of Piero's villa. He remembered, the first time he had gone through it, that wonderful feeling of entering an enchanted place, a place of legend.

He walked up to the gate and pressed the small brass button next to the old nameplate without a name. After at least a minute, the entryphone crackled. "Yes?"

Nico recognised Maria's voice.

"It's Nico," he said, lowering his head towards the entry-phone. The childlike euphoria he had felt earlier seemed to have gradually been dissipating, and to have vanished completely the moment his index finger had touched the brass button.

"Oh, great!" the entryphone crackled. "Come in!"

The huge gate trembled and started to open. There's always something magical, something grand, Nico thought, in seeing a big gate open onto a private drive.

When Nico reached the top of the drive, Maria was already waiting for him in front of the big dark wooden door. It had been many months, possibly years, since he had last set foot in the villa, and he wondered how it was possible for it to look bigger each time he saw it.

Maria was even more beautiful than Nico remembered. She was wearing a pair of dark linen trousers which would have looked overly large on anyone else, her feet were bare, and above the trousers she had on a simple white blouse knotted at the waist, with the sleeves rolled up. The top buttons of her blouse were undone, giving a glimpse of the curve of her breasts, and her dark hair was pulled back and loosely held.

"Hi," Nico said, pausing at the foot of the stone steps that led up to the front door.

"Hi," Maria replied, with what seemed to him for a moment like a knowing air.

Nico wondered how it was that some people managed to appear elegant and charming even when they should have looked scruffy. He wondered if there were special courses for it, or if it was simply something in the genes.

Nico climbed the steps and let Maria embrace him. He realised it could well be the first time this had happened. In the more than twenty years that he'd been friends with Piero, it was the first time his sister had come within a metre of him.

"You're looking good," Maria said, freeing herself from the embrace and looking Nico up and down.

"You, too," Nico said, smiling. Maria smiled at him again with that odd hint of mischief and turned to go inside the house.

"Thanks for coming so quickly. We're really at the end of our tether. Who knows, maybe with you here … "

"Don't mention it," Nico said. He would have liked to say something more intelligent, but he couldn't think of anything at the moment. All he wanted was to be taken to Piero and finally see how things really were. "Where is he?" he asked.

Maria turned and looked at him for a moment with an embarrassed smile. "He's upstairs," she said. "But mother said she'd like to see you first."

Nico had no wish to see Piero's mother, especially now. "Of course," he said. "Me, too."

Maria again gave an embarrassed smile and suddenly turned and tiptoed to the sitting room.

Through the big French window, the reddish light of sunset flooded the huge frescoed room, full of colourful abstract paintings and leather sofas. The whole room had a thick orange-yellow colour which did not match the furnishings and gave it an awkward air. And there in the middle, sitting up against the armrest of one of the big sofas, was the tiny figure of Piero's mother, busy embroidering something.

"Mother," Maria said, without expression.

The little woman raised her head and looked at her daughter gravely, then shifted her eyes to Nico. After a couple of seconds, her face broadened in a big smile and she stood up. "Nicola, darling!" she cried, opening her arms wide. "What an absolute pleasure it is to have you here! Let me give you a kiss."

Nico smiled as best he could and walked towards her. "Hello, Miriam," he said when they were close.

Piero's mother put her hands out and drew Nico's face to her to kiss him. "What a lovely surprise!" she said, boring into his brain with eyes that were too wide. "Piero will be happy."

"I just happened to be in the area," Nico said.

Piero's mother nodded, again smiling broadly. "You did absolutely the right thing! Now tell me about yourself. Are you still working in the theatre?"

Nico had never worked in the theatre.

"Yes, of course," he said. "It's tough work, but someone has to do it." He had always dreamt of saying that sentence, but had never found the opportunity before. Now, though, seemed the perfect time.

Piero's mother burst out laughing and gave him a pinch on the cheek, then turned to Maria. "How sweet he is!" she said. Then she turned back to Nico. "And you're still a … "

"Lighting technician," Nico said.

"How nice! Did you hear that, Maria?"

Nico nodded, pursing his lips. Maria looked at him and at her mother and frowned.

Piero's mother kept looking at Nico and smiling, Nico kept nodding, and Maria looked from one to the other a couple of times. Then Nico looked around the room.

"Everything's still the same, I see," he said.

"Yes!" Piero's mother cried, her voice pitched too high. "Just like the old days!"

Maria put a hand on her mother's arm.

"Such good times," Miriam said, her voice trailing away.

Nico wondered which time Miriam was thinking of most: the time she had thrown him out of the house, beating him with a broomstick as she did so, or the time she had categorically forbidden Piero to see him.

"Yes," Nico said. "Good times."

There were a few more seconds of silence.

"Why don't I go and see Piero?" Nico said, turning to Maria. "What do you think?"

"But of course!" Miriam said. "Maria, will you go with him?" She turned back to Nico. "He'll be so pleased to see you."

For a moment, it occurred to Nico that this was all a joke, and, as Maria walked ahead of him out of the room, he felt the impulse to look round for hidden cameras and fake mirrors.

Maria led him back into the wide entrance hall and up the dark wooden staircase. After a few steps, she turned her head slightly to one side. "You know," she said, "she still doesn't know how to handle it."

Nico looked at her without a word for a couple of seconds, and suddenly wondered if inside that wonderful creature there was actually a person. "Obviously," he said.

At the top of the stairs, Maria turned right into a long corridor and stopped outside Piero's room, the same room where Nico had slept dozens of times.

"Here we are," Maria said, and she placed her hand on the dark steel handle. For a moment Nico looked at Maria with a touch of embarrassed anxiety, and she gave a slight smile in response. Then Maria knocked lightly on the door and started to open it.

"Piero?" she said softly. "You have a visitor. Come and see. Nico's here."

The door, which still had a few Kiss and Depeche Mode stickers on it, opened to reveal the cream-coloured rugs, the single bed, the dark shelves full of discs, books and trinkets and the big window at the far end leading to the little terrace.

And there, behind the bed, in front of the window, backlit by the rays of the sunset, was a crouching figure, fiddling with something on the floor. Piero turned to look at Nico and Maria. He stuck his lips out in an O, grunted two or three times, his head swaying, screwed up his face and slapped his forehead twice. Then he looked down at the floor again and his body rocked slightly from side to side.

Nico stood there for a few seconds, looking gravely from a distance at what had once been his friend. "Hi," he said at last.

Maria looked at Nico, her eyes on the verge of tears, as he stepped forwards into the room.

Nico walked past the bed and approached Piero. He was naked, crouching beside the bed, playing with a little pile of pistachio shells, just like a monkey. Piero looked up, and for a moment his mouth stretched, showing all his teeth, then he immediately looked down again, grunted and stuck two fingers in the little pile of shells.

"Hi, Piero," Nico said.

Piero again looked up, smiling in that lopsided way, and immediately looked down again. Then he waddled on his arms and legs, nudged Nico's leg with his shoulder and, grunting, went straight back to his place in front of the little pile of shells.

"It may be best if I leave you two alone," Maria said, from the door.

Nico turned and looked at her. Her eyes were sad, and there was an embarrassed half-smile on her lips.

"Yes," Nico said. "It may be best."

Maria left the room, pulling the door shut behind her. Nico watched as she disappeared and stood there for a few seconds staring at the closed door. When he turned again to look at Piero, his friend was trying to make a shape out of the pistachio shells.

One of the last times they had spoken on the phone, Piero had been in London on business and had asked Nico to come up and join him.

"I can't now," Nico said. "You come down here."

"Shit, Nico, I'd really like that. I'd like to come down there and just mess around for a few days without thinking of anything. Why don't we go away together?"

Nico laughed. "Piero," he said, "you've been saying the same thing since you were twelve. But where the fuck do you want to go?"

"I don't know. Somewhere. Australia, for instance."

"Are you turning gay?"

"No, but I'm thinking of it. Why?"

"Because that's the kind of offer you usually make a woman. Look, I'm not giving you my arse."

Piero laughed at that. "It would be nice, though," he said.

"What, having my arse?"

"That, too. No, I meant dropping everything and going away."

Nico thought about it for a moment. "But do you really have to go to Australia to drop everything?"

Piero, too, thought for a moment. "No, maybe not. But Australia's cool."

"Why?"

"Because of the waves."

"How do you mean?"

"I mean the surfing."

"Piero, you can't surf."

"I know, but I can always learn."

"Fuck off," Nico said.

"And also because there aren't so many people there."

"Now that's a good reason."

"A very good reason, I think."

"Yes, a very good reason."

For a few moments, neither of them had said a word, then Piero said, "Nico?"

"Yes?"

"Whatever happened to our dreams?"

"Dreams? What dreams?"

"I don't know, but we must have had some."

"My dream was to own a Panda four-by-four."

"And?"

"And now I own a Panda four-by-four."

Piero gave a faint, unconvinced laugh and fell silent again. "Oh, well," he said after a while.

"Piero," Nico said, "the people who came before us fucked up our dreams."

Piero had been silent for a couple of seconds, then said, "Maybe we should have lived in the Seventies."

"Yes, then we would have been disappointed. We're better off, we were born disappointed and that's it."

"Oh, well," Piero said again.

"Piero?" Nico said.

"Yes?"

"I think you just need a good sandwich."

"You may be right," Piero said.

Nico lowered himself until he was sitting next to Piero with his back against the bed. After a few seconds, Piero grunted a couple of times and pushed a handful of pistachio shells towards Nico. Nico moved his hand over them and lowered his head, trying to look his friend in the eyes. Piero stuck his lips out again and slapped his forehead twice with his hand, then calmly arranged four shells in a line, swaying slightly.

Nico watched him screw up his face and grunt, then he moved two of the shells towards Piero's line and put them on the side, as if to start a new line at right angles to the first. Piero grunted again and slapped his head with his hand, then waddled to one side, pivoting on his feet, and added two shells to the new line. At last, a square appeared.

They carried on like this for a while. Piero would put down a shell and Nico would move another shell closer to it, then Piero would add another, and so on until a shape emerged, a star or a circle or whatever, and they would continue until the strange shell design was complete. Then Piero would grunt, slap his head with his hands and smile in the same monkey way, screwing up his face and showing his teeth. A couple of times he laid his head for a moment on Nico's shoulder. The last time Piero had done that was at least ten years earlier as they came out of a club—he was completely drunk and joked to Nico that he should take him home.

After about an hour, Nico put his hand on Piero's bare shoulder and told him he had to go. Piero did not look up, but scratched behind his ear and grunted twice, more softly this time. Nico sat there for a few seconds, looking at Piero with his hand resting on his shoulder, then looked to one side for a moment and stood up.

He looked at him one last time as he was leaving the room, with his hand still on the door handle. The sun had been down for a while, and the electric light made everything even more absurd.

When Nico started to walk downstairs, he saw Maria sitting at the foot of the stairs.

"Well?" Maria said when Nico had come closer, looking up at him without standing. "How did you find him?"

Nico slowly walked down two more steps, with his hands in his pockets. "Well," he said, "he's acting like a monkey."

Maria stared at him without saying anything. She seemed a little disappointed. "Yes, but ... "

"I don't know, Maria," Nico said. "I really don't know. The last time we spoke on the phone he was complaining about his work and now he's acting like a monkey. I don't know. I really don't know."

Maria continued looking at him without saying anything.

"Would you call me a taxi, please?" Nico said.

"Of course," Maria said, rising and half smiling. "But I can give you a lift if you like," she added once she was on her feet.

"No, thanks, a taxi will be fine. Really."

"As you wish." Maria climbed down the last two steps and turned. "Will you come back tomorrow?"

Nico looked at her and took a moment to reconnect. "Of course. I'd be glad to."

Maria nodded, smiling. She walked back into the drawing room, went to the telephone and picked up the receiver.

Piero's mother was still there, embroidering with an almost military determination. After a few seconds she looked up at her daughter, and saw Nico.

"Hello!" she cried. She put the embroidery to one side and looked at Nico with those over-wide eyes. "Well? How did you find him?"

Nico managed to squeeze out a smile. "Fine," he nodded.

"Really? I think he's in good shape, too!"

"Yes, I agree."

"Are you staying for a few days?"

"Oh, yes, it looks as if I'll be staying the whole week-end."

"How nice! Piero will be glad! Perhaps the two of you could go out for a meal or a drink the way you used to. I'm sure he'd love that."

Nico wondered which was worse: that Miriam should pretend nothing was wrong now, or that she had always done so before.

"Yes, maybe," he said. "We'll see how it goes."

"Or you could go the cinema. You always liked that."

"Right," Nico said. "It's an idea."

Maria put down the phone and walked up to Nico. "The taxi will be here in five minutes," she said.

Nico had never appreciated a taxi so much in his life.

"What, are you going already?" Piero's mother asked, frowning sadly.

"Afraid so," Nico said. "It's late and I haven't even told my parents I'm coming."

"What a pity," Piero's mother said. "I was hoping you might be able to have dinner with us."

"Yes, I know. Another time, perhaps."

"All right, but we'll see you again while you're here."

"Of course, Miriam. I'll be back tomorrow as early as I can, I promise. Keep well."

"Thank you, darling. You, too."

Miriam picked up her embroidery as if nothing had happened, and after a moment Nico followed Maria out of the room.

"Why don't you wait here?" she asked at the door.

"No, thanks, I'll go and wait at the gate. I like walking."

"It's up to you," Maria said. "I'll see you tomorrow."

"Sure," Nico said, then went up to Maria, let her kiss him twice on the cheeks and walked out.

When he heard the door close behind him, he felt as though someone had stuck an oxygen mask over his face, and the air outside had never seemed so scented.

NICO GOT IN THE TAXI and gave his parents' address, then sat close to the window looking out at the road rushing past, trying not to think about the strangest thing he had ever experienced in his life.

The car passed the big bend, and Nico remembered all the times he and Piero had passed it on mopeds, racing to see which of them could take it faster, the time he had skidded and smashed the moped into the low wall, all the times they had stopped here at dawn, returning from some night out, and leant over to look down at the town and smoke their last cigarettes, and the time Piero had fallen. Then he decided he didn't really want to remember those things right now, and he started looking out again, concentrating on the road and the cars rushing past.

That afternoon, on the train, Nico had thought it might be nice to call home and announce his arrival, but then he had decided that he didn't want to—that it would be amusing to turn up like that at the last moment, like the wandering, unpredictable son he had never been.

The taxi driver, who was all smiles, dropped him outside his house. There was a breeze now, and the air felt cooler. Nico slid a hand through the bars of the little gate and stretched until he found the button that released the lock. He looked around to see if anyone was watching him. That was something he always enjoyed doing, as if knowing that little secret made him automatically feel at home, especially as what he was doing was vaguely fraudulent.

Nico went through the gate, climbed the few steps leading to the front door and rang the bell. He heard some indistinct noises inside the house, and his mother's muffled voice saying something as she came to the door.

When Nico's mother opened the door, the sight of him almost took her breath away. She was wearing a stained apron with red and white stripes.

"Who? … "

She was licking her fingers, and she froze with her hand in mid-air and her mouth open. Nico wondered if she was simply surprised or also a little bit agitated.

"Hi, Mum, I'm your son. Remember me?"

Nico's mother took a couple of seconds to reconnect and get her hand and everything else moving again. "Darling! What a surprise! What are you doing here?"

Behind his mother, Nico saw a man rush stark naked across the entrance hall and up the stairs.

Nico opened his eyes wide for a moment and looked anxiously at his mother. "Mum, why did Dad just run upstairs naked?"

Nico's mother raised her eyebrows, turned round with feigned curiosity, then turned back to her son and gave him a lovely smile. "I imagine he was going up to get dressed, darling."

It seemed to Nico that he didn't have time for that.

"What shall I do?" he asked, pretending to smile questioningly. "Can I come in?"

"Oh, God, darling, I'm sorry! It's just … you know … "

Nico left his jacket in the hall and followed his mother into the kitchen. She was making something strange in the wok—that strange, wonderful concave oriental pan that ought to have produced only exquisite delicacies, but didn't seem to produce anything very much in the hands of Nico's mother. Nico tried to remember when exactly it was that his mother had been seized by that obsession with all things oriental, but couldn't really pin it down.

144

All he knew was that overnight the house had started to fill with strange books with dark-blue paper and red ideograms, extravagant kitchen utensils and gardening tools, colourful leaflets with exotic names on them, batik sarongs and hemp skirts. Nico remembered talking about it to his sister.

"Do you think this oriental kick of Mum's is normal?" he had asked her one day over the phone.

"What do you mean?"

"You know, all these books about the Orient and Zen and Japanese cooking, all that kind of thing."

"What of it?"

"I don't know, don't you think it's strange?"

"Nico, let her do what she wants," his sister had said.

Nico wondered if his dad being naked in the living room had something to do with the same cultural revolution, or if he had started smoking dope.

"Mum," Nico said, "do Dad and you smoke dope?"

For a moment Nico's mother stopped what she was doing—stirring a dark mixture of sorry-looking vegetables in her wok—and looked at her son with a puzzled half-smile. "No, darling. Why? What makes you think that?"

"No reason. It's been a long day. I'm sorry."

She stroked his cheek. Nico was sitting on the high iron stool next to the ovens, as he had when he was a child, nibbling at pieces of food left over from his mother's experiments.

"Don't worry," she said, then started stirring the vegetables again. "Will this be enough?" she asked after a while, pensively.

Silently, Nico lifted his eyebrows and pursed his lips.

"I don't think it is," she said. "I think I should add a little more spaghetti."

Nico craned his neck to look in the wok and wondered which of those sorry-looking ingredients came under the admittedly vague heading of spaghetti.

His mother looked at Nico and stroked his face again. "What a nice surprise," she said, then went back to stirring the spaghetti and the vegetables. "But what are you doing here?" she asked, and there was something slightly different, almost inquisitorial, in her tone.

"Piero has started acting like a monkey."

"Mm," said Nico's mother. "How nice."

Nico gave his mother a puzzled look. "Not really," he said.

"Oh," his mother said. Then she stopped for a moment. "I'm sorry, in what way?"

"Some time this summer he suddenly flipped and started acting like a monkey."

"What do you mean, 'like a monkey'?"

"Like a monkey: he crouches on the ground, grunts and smiles in a lopsided way like a chimpanzee."

Nico's mother looked at her son with her mouth open in surprise, and Nico caught himself thinking that it was her most genuine expression since she had opened the door. Then she started stirring the vegetables again.

"I always said he was a strange boy," she said.

Nico would have liked to say that being strange was one thing, damn it, but starting to act like a monkey was quite another matter, then it struck him that it wasn't worth it, he didn't want to talk about it anyway, he was rather tired and this whole business of Piero and the monkey was perhaps too straightforward to require much discussion.

After a few minutes, Nico's father came into the kitchen. He was himself again: he had put on his usual jacket and tie and light-brown trousers. He had gone back to being the aloof, distinguished man Nico had always known. Nico told himself not to think about the fact that only a little while earlier he had seen him run upstairs naked.

"Hello, son."

His father came up to Nico and they kissed each other lightly on the cheek.

"Hello, Dad."

"Everything OK?"

"Yes, not bad. And you?"

"Pretty good. How's work?"

"Fine, really. Just fine."

"Great."

Silence.

"I'm going to watch the news," Nico's father said.

Nico nodded, and his father left the kitchen, taking a small piece of bread with him. Nico's mother suggested it might be nice if they all ate in the kitchen, just like in the old days, so Nico got down off the stool and laid three places on the wooden breakfast bar beside the cooker. Over dinner, they talked of this and that as they tried to get his mother's mixture down them. His father made another attempt to show an interest in his son's work, and Nico tried to involve him, too, in the Piero thing, but without much success.

When dinner was over, his mother put the dishes in the dishwasher and they went into the living room to see what was on TV. They all sat down on the sofa, with Nico in the middle. From time to time he turned his head slightly to look at his parents and see if they, too, felt the same kind of cheerful self-consciousness, and they looked at him briefly in return, but then turned back to the TV as if nothing had happened.

After just over half-an-hour, Nico told himself it had been quite a day, stood up and told his parents that he was going to bed. His mother looked up with an affectionate half-smile and told him his bed was ready, with clean sheets and everything.

"Just like the old days," she said, still smiling.

Nico wondered why they were all so obsessed with the old days. He nodded pensively a couple of times, then turned and walked upstairs.

His room was indeed just as it had been, with the Moana Pozzi and Rolling Stones posters and the photo of Tom Waits on the wall, together with all the other teenage nonsense no one had had the courage to take down in all these years.

Nico started wandering around the room, moving a few ornaments and picking up a few magazines. He saw the old issue of *Playboy* with which he had come for the first time. He leafed through it until he found the photo of Anna Nicole Smith that had caused that miracle, and for a moment he felt like making a real leap into the old days and going to the bathroom to masturbate over his first woman. Then it occurred to him that he was too tired and disorientated even for that. He undressed and went to the bathroom to clean his teeth.

In the wardrobe, he found an old T-shirt to sleep in. He slid under the blankets and for a few seconds lay there, looking at his room, thinking of all the times he had looked at it from the same angle and how different it seemed now.

He reached out his arm towards the bedside table, picked up the telephone and tried to call his agent. Still off the hook. Maybe it was just as well, he thought: if it was on and she had answered, she might have bawled him out for calling her at this hour, and Nico didn't really want that.

He put the phone down and dialled another number.

"Hello?"

"So, wanker, how's it going?"

"Hi, dumbo. Fine, and you?"

It was like music, hearing a sane, normal, calm voice that didn't change and didn't make animal noises.

"Oh, not bad. Same old same old."

"What the fuck are you doing here?"

"I'll tell you later. What are you doing tomorrow?"

"I don't know, no plans for the moment."

"How about having a bite to eat?"

"Where?"

"Oh, I don't know. How about Vinaino's?"

"Vinaino's, great. Shall I meet you there?"

"Fine. One o'clock?"

"One o'clock."

"Bye, arsehole."

"Bye, dumbo."

Nico put down the phone and put it back on the bedside table, then had second thoughts, picked it up again and dialled another number.

The phone rang at the other end, and for a moment Nico hoped that no one would answer.

"Hello?"

"Hi, darling."

"Hi."

Giada sounded tired and a bit depressed, and for a moment, improbably, Nico felt a slight sense of guilt.

"How are you?" he asked.

"Quite well. And you?"

Nico stretched out a bit more in bed. "I'm not sure. Fine, I think. It's been a long day."

"Yes, I know. For me, too."

Nico wondered if there was some subtext in those words, then decided he didn't care. "We should play a game of squash."

"Squash?"

"Yes, you know, that game where you bang a ball like crazy against a wall?"

"I know what squash is, but what's that got to do with anything?"

"I don't know, they say you sweat a lot."

"Have you ever played it?"

"No."

"So how do you know what it's like?"

"I don't know, it's always struck me as one of those cool things you do in the evening to wind down. One of those stupid things actually, because when you think about it, banging a ball against a wall is a pretty strange way to wind down."

Giada gave a half-laugh. "Silly," she said.

It was nice to hear her say that, Nico thought. It had been a while since that had last happened.

"How's your friend?" Giada asked.

Nico thought about it for a moment. "You have an amazing voice."

"What?"

"You have an amazing voice."

"Oh," Giada said. "Have you only just realised?"

"No, I mean tonight. You have an amazing voice tonight."

"Why, how is it usually?"

"No, usually it's very nice, but tonight … Anyway."

Silence. Nico felt like sighing, but decided not to.

"But what about your friend?"

"Well," Nico said, "my friend is acting like a monkey."

"You mean, really?"

"Yes, really. He grunts and slaps his own head just like a monkey. It's quite impressive."

"My God."

"But he doesn't seem that bad."

Giada said nothing for a moment and Nico tried to imagine what position she was in.

"Oh, well," Giada said.

Another silence. It was if both of them wanted to say something, but were too tired.

"Talk to you tomorrow?"

"Tomorrow, sure."

"Sleep well."

"You, too."

M ARCO WAS ONE OF THOSE PEOPLE who for some reason reach a point in their lives when they seem to realise something other people haven't, and are constantly demonstrating the fact with a serenity they can't conceal. After finishing school, he had tried university for a while, then had decided it wasn't for him and had started doing all kinds of little jobs to make a living and save enough money for a plane ticket. His first destination had been South America. He had left one Thursday morning and had not returned for months.

That was how he lived: wandering from job to job, from country to country, finding what work he could and putting aside a few lire. Whenever he grew tired of it, he would start to get restless again, the way people who travel a lot tend to do. Then something had changed. Overnight, he had reappeared in town, and Nico had immediately realised that he was different from the other times. He had started working in a restaurant and after less than a year had become manager of a grocery store.

His life had suddenly become all about salami and bread and cold cuts for lunch and white shirts and jokes with the ladies who came there every day to do their shopping. Nico had often wondered what had happened, where Marco had found that thing which had stopped his heart beating too fast and given him the calm and serenity of someone who has realised something that other people haven't. Nico had wondered where he had found that thing; if it was somewhere in the South Seas, or in the mountains of New Zealand, or if quite simply he had found it in the ham he cut day after day. Nico had even promised himself that he would ask him one day where he had found that thing. But then it always turned out that he never did anything, it always turned out that even just the idea of asking the question made him feel stupid.

When Marco arrived, Nico was sitting on a moped reading the last pages of the newspaper. He had got up late, and after chatting a bit with his parents had come down into town and slowly made his way to Vinaino's, where he had arranged to meet Marco, stopping first at a news-stand, then at a café, where he had had a nice breakfast sitting out in the sun.

"Hey," Marco said.

Nico put down the newspaper and looked at his friend, raising his eyebrows. "Hey," he said.

"So?" Marco asked.

"So what?"

"Are we going to stand here all day like idiots, looking into each other's eyes?"

Nico looked at him a moment longer, then he smiled and got off the moped. "Let's go," he said.

They walked along the street for about fifty metres until they got to a small restaurant with a wooden façade and four tables outside on the pavement, on a platform.

A distinguished-looking lady who looked a bit out of place there greeted them as if she had known them for ages and seated them at one of the outdoor tables. They sat down opposite each other and ordered a bottle of wine.

"House wine will be fine," Marco said.

Nico passed his hand over his face. "How are things?" he asked.

"Oh, not bad. Usual stuff."

Nico gave a half-laugh. "And Anna?"

"Fine. She's at home with the kid. She wanted to come and say hello to you, but she was dead tired."

"Why?"

"We were up late last night."

"Doing what?"

"That's our business. And you?"

"No, I wasn't up late last night. I had dinner with my parents and talked a load of crap. When I arrived, my father was naked in the living room. What do you think that means?"

"How you mean, 'naked in the living room'?"

"I don't know. When my mum opened the door, I saw him zoom upstairs stark naked."

"Your dad."

"I swear."

"I thought he even wore a tie to take a shower."

Nico gave another half-laugh. "Apparently not."

"And what the hell was he doing walking naked around the house?"

"I don't know. What do you think?"

"Who knows, maybe your folks were … "

"All right, I get the picture, let's drop it."

Marco gave a half-laugh. "Poor guys, though."

"Why?"

"They can't even do what they want to in their own house without some pain in the arse turning up."

"Yes, like their son."

"For instance."

"It's funny, though."

"What is?"

"I always wondered how they've managed to stay together all these years."

"What's that got to do with it?"

"Now it doesn't seem so strange any more."

"Just because you saw your dad run upstairs naked?"

"Yes."

"I don't follow you."

Nico took a piece of bread and put it in his mouth and looked Marco in the eyes, trying to sort out what he wanted to say.

"It's as if I'd realised that my father was actually quite a different person, someone who runs around the house naked for instance. That means by now he could be anyone, even the kind of person who'd manage to stay with my mother for thirty-five years."

Marco looked at Nico for a couple of seconds with raised eyebrows. "Go to hell," he said.

Nico smiled and turned to the lady, who had approached their table with a notepad in her hand. They both ordered roast loin of pork with potatoes, then sat sipping their wine.

Nico played with the breadcrumbs for a moment. "Piero has started acting like a monkey," he said.

Marco was silent and still behind his big sunglasses.

"I'm telling the truth," Nico said.

"What do you mean, 'like a monkey'?"

"This summer he was with his sister and apparently one day he just bent double and started acting like a monkey. At first they all laughed, but then he wouldn't stop. That's why I'm here. Maria called me yesterday and asked me if I could come and visit him, to see if he was getting any better."

"Have you seen him?"

"I saw him yesterday afternoon."

"And how is he?" Marco asked, taking off his sunglasses.

"Impressive. He's just like a monkey. He grunts and slaps his head and crouches on the floor playing with pistachio shells."

"Pistachio shells?"

"Yes, he piles them up and makes shapes. I joined in for a while."

"You and Piero played with pistachio shells?" Marco's face twisted in what looked like a grimace of pain.

Nico nodded. "Yes."

Marco looked at him for a couple of seconds. "Are you sure you're not bullshitting me?"

"I've never been more serious," Nico said, and started playing with the breadcrumbs again. "The strange thing is, when Maria called me I assumed it wasn't true. Or rather, not that it wasn't true: as if it was something amusing; something weird and cool to talk about. But when I went in that room and saw him … "

"What?"

"I don't know. He really seemed like a monkey."

"But what the hell does it mean?"

"I don't know what it means, Marco. I haven't the faintest idea. I only know it was quite a blow."

After lunch Marco offered to take Nico to Piero's house. They climbed up into the hills in the old blue Fiat 500 that had once been his mother's.

"Sure you don't want to come in?" Nico asked when they were outside Piero's gate, just before getting out of the car.

"I don't think so," Marco said. "Maybe tomorrow."

Nico nodded.

"Say hello to them for me," Marco said.

"Sure," Nico said.

"And don't worry."

"OK."

Nico shook Marco's hand, got out of the car, watched his friend drive away, then walked to the gate.

He put his hands on the grey, slightly blistered paint. Once that gate had been green, then it had been brown, and finally grey like now. Nico remembered the few times over the years when he had seen the gate all orange, covered in anti-rust paint. That was something that had always made him feel good. It was as if that orange paint gave objects a kind of grandeur. Ever since he was a child, he had told himself that he, too, would like to paint something orange one day.

For a while, he stood there, hanging on the bars of the gate, moving his hands over the little blisters in the paint. In places, rust was starting to show. He looked through the bars. The drive rose between the trees until it disappeared round the bend. Somewhere there, at the end of the drive, were Miriam and Maria and Piero and that mass of unspoken things that burnt like hot coals.

Nico turned and started to walk back down the road. He would pass the big bend and carry on down into town; he would walk along the avenues and through the centre; he would reach the station and get on the first train. Once he arrived, he might start walking again, down to the river and up again and all the way across the city, until he got home. In the evening he might cook himself a quick dish of pasta, take the phone off the hook and put on a good film, then go to bed and try not to think about anything.